A. M. Stirling

THIRTEEN

Best wishes, Maggie

Much Love

Mike x

WOMBACH
PRESS

For Martha

Design and typesetting by Wayne Gamble

Printed and bound in the UK by
Martins the Printers, Berwick-upon-Tweed

ISBN: 978-1-9161601-2-5 (paperback)
978-1-9161601-3-2 (eBook)

WOMBACH PRESS
wombachpress@gmail.com

About the Author

A.M. Stirling is a nom de plume. After a career as a photographer and academic he began writing fiction in 2010. The psychological thriller *Bad Magic* was published by Wombach Press in 2019. He also writes under his own name, Mike Golding.

'Spitfire' first appeared in *Uncommonalities IV*, from Bratum Books, 'Flora and Fauna' in *Impspired Magazine*, Volume Fourteen, and 'The Dark Wood' in *Thin Skin, Issue 3*, all credited as Mike Golding.

Contents

Art's My Thing

The house is too big. I know that. There's a room overlooking the garden, which was probably intended to be a nursery. I had the idea of turning it into a study, with a desk and some bookshelves, but it never came to anything. In the end I had the walls painted pure white, and this is where I keep Anna's painting. Out of sight, and not on show. David thinks I'm ashamed of it, or don't like it any more, but he's wrong on both counts.

Art's my thing, you see. Paintings. I look at them, read about them, and I collect them. We have a Derwatt, which I bought years ago, before all the hoo-hah. Now, as things turned out, it was a very good investment. So no, David doesn't mind about the money.

I'm an art tourist: all the major cities, all the big exhibitions, Venice for the Biennale, Kassel for Documenta. All of it. But it's not just the big names. I like to poke about the private galleries, the ones you need a map to find, and I go to the student shows every year. I'm always on the look-out for something interesting. In fact, I'm known for it.

I'd gone to an opening at The Lucy Vane Gallery. Lucy billed it as 'The Summer Show' but it was just a ragbag of work she hadn't managed to sell. A clearance sale, in other words, and nothing I hadn't seen before. The crowd was thinner than usual, less enthusiastic. I cruised the room, making idle chitchat, while the gallery assistants buzzed around with bottles, topping up our glasses.

I was on my third glass when Lucy caught up with me. She kissed me on the cheek.

'Are you selling anything?' I said.

'Don't ask. It's the summer.'

'I know. All anyone can talk about is how much a euro's worth.'

'Something to show you,' she said, winking.

Now, Lucy's such a hustler, and she made a big thing of taking me into the storeroom at the back of the gallery. A large painting was leaning against the wall on wooden blocks, its wrapping discarded on the floor. Even under the fluorescent lights it looked remarkable. To be honest, I found it difficult to take my eyes off it.

'It's interesting,' I said.

'I'd like to use the word 'shamanistic' but I don't know if the market would bear it,' said Lucy.

'Who's the artist?'

'Anna Morgan. I found her in Berlin last year. You know, on one of my little trips.'

She leaned against the storage rack, idly picking at some bubble wrap with her fingernail, and asked if I'd like to see more. When I nodded, she called one of the gallery assistants to come and pull out another painting. I was enjoying the theatrics, and Lucy was pleased; our little game had begun.

A couple of months later, at the opening of the gallery's next exhibition, I'd barely a glass of wine in my hand before Lucy ambushed me. I knew she would; I hadn't bought the painting yet. Of course, we both knew I was going to buy it, but the game was still in play.

'Verity,' she said, 'I have a surprise for you. Come and meet Anna Morgan.'

And there she was, about thirty and attractive in a quirky sort of way, dressed in a white linen shirt with three-quarter sleeves. She wore bright red lipstick. Everything else was black: trousers, jewellery, shoes, and her hair, which was cut into a short, severe bob. As I shook her hand, I was struck by the smell of her; perfume and tobacco smoke.

She had an anxious expression and couldn't settle. Her hands fluttered down at her sides, reached up to adjust her hair, first one side, then the other. These obsessive movements were compelling. The more I looked, the more I saw. Her fingernails, red to match her lips, were bitten down to the quick and the varnish chipped. On her left forearm, barely hidden by the sleeve, was a series of short, parallel scars. Her anxiety was palpable.

'Verity has actually seen some of your work,' said Lucy. 'Remember, I told you?'

'Oh,' said Anna, 'you're the collector.'

And I said that was a bit grand because I just had a few good pieces. Now, I'll admit I was being modest, but I got the impression Anna was disappointed.

'So, how do you decide what to buy?' she said, without meeting my eye.

'Well, I know it sounds like an awful cliché, but I know what I like.'

'It is a cliché,' said Anna. 'But when you buy a painting, it should appeal to your heart. That's all there is to it.'

Lucy made an excuse and left us alone, hoping that by 'getting to know the artist' I might hurry up and sign the cheque. Anna just stood in front of me and said nothing. I looked over her shoulder, across the gallery, at the small groups of people talking, laughing and draining their glasses. She followed my gaze.

'Do you know all those people?'

'Most of them.'

'Art lovers,' she said. 'You can tell.'

I didn't know if she meant to be ironic. It was true, hardly anyone was looking at the paintings, but they were selling. The little red dots on the walls next to them attested to that. Now, it isn't good form to say so out loud, but I didn't like the work. It was gestural abstract painting and it left me cold. Anna's reticence made me feel awkward. I said the first thing that came into my head.

'I really loathe this work.'

'It's bloody awful,' she said. 'It's so masculine, isn't it? Pushing the paint around to show it who's boss.'

'It's the art world equivalent of Heavy Metal.'

'How so?'

'Too much noise,' I said, and she laughed.

Anna smiled at me. The tension that had emanated from her, that I had found so alarming, dissipated. It was a strange thing, but I wanted to protect her, to hold out my hand to her. I invited her for dinner. What else could I do?

*

Anna was late. When I opened the door to her she stood with her face lowered, looking up at me like a child who's been caught out. She'd been drinking, and reeked of tobacco smoke.

She said, 'You have such a beautiful home.' But it sounded flat, as if she thought it was the thing to say. As if she'd rehearsed it. To put her at ease, I told her she was welcome. But I did more than that; I embraced her and kissed her on both cheeks.

Anna began to look at the paintings in the hall.

'You have a Derwatt. Oh, Verity, you are a real collector.'

She studied the painting, and I watched her looking. Completely absorbed, she didn't realise there were other guests. We heard laughter from the sitting room, and she stiffened like a startled rabbit.

'Come on,' I said, guiding her through the door. 'They won't bite.'

Lucy was there with her husband Mark who runs a recruitment business. There had to be someone to make up the numbers. I'd asked Catherine, who works for Lucy. Siobhan and Chris were there too. Siobhan is my oldest friend, so they always come, rain or shine. Anna sat on the edge of one of the settees, drinking her gin and tonic too quickly.

When the time came, I ushered everyone into the dining room. For a starter I'd made *cèpes à la génoise* using a mixture of wild mushrooms I'd gathered myself that morning. Foraging for mushrooms is another one of my 'enthusiasms' as David calls them. I go out into the country with a hazel basket, one of those special Opinel knives with a brush at the end of the handle, and a field guide.

'It's a wonderful idea,' said Anna. 'Isn't it dangerous, though?' She looked down at her plate, in mock or real concern, I couldn't tell. 'I mean you might pick a poisonous one by mistake.'

'There's no chance of that. I've been doing it for a very long time,' I said, holding up crossed fingers. 'No fatalities, yet. And to be honest, I've got a book with some very good photographs in it.'

After the main course, salt-baked lamb shanks, I decided we should have a break before dessert. I cleared the plates, and David refreshed everyone's glass.

'I hear you're a painter, Anna,' said Siobhan.

'Yes,' she said, 'I am.'

She left it there and everyone around the table paused, expecting her to say more. After a moment, the men started to talk about football or cars, I can't really remember which, but Siobhan persisted.

'And what are your paintings like?'

'Anna's paintings are exquisite,' I said.

'Haven't you just moved here?' said Siobhan, always wanting to know the ins and outs of everything, and never quite knowing when to give up.

'Yes.'

'Where have you come from?'

'Well, I've been in Berlin,' said Anna. 'Why are you so interested in my life?'

'Because I envy you,' said Siobhan. 'Now the kids have grown up, I've started painting. I'm going to classes.'

'A lot of women do that at your age. You must be feeling a need to get in touch with your creative side.'

'Oh, yes. You're right. Bringing up a family is a wonderful thing, but you end up putting your own interests on the back burner. Now I've got the time, how did you put it? To get in touch with my creative side.'

'All that art stuff costs a fortune, doesn't it?' said Chris. 'I know, because I'm paying for it.'

'Anna, can I ask you?' said Siobhan. 'How do you decide what to paint? That's what I'm not sure of.'

'Well, it's not like going shopping with your husband's credit card,' said Anna, standing up and knocking the table. The cutlery rattled and the wine glasses trembled.

She said she was sorry but she had to go for a cigarette. I watched as she went out through the French doors. It was getting dark outside, and the brightness of the room was reflected in the glass, but I saw Anna clearly enough, standing under a cloud of blue grey smoke in the middle of the lawn.

Siobhan turned to me and raised her eyebrows.

'It must be the artistic temperament,' she said, trying to give her voice an edge.

Remembering the pale white scars I'd glimpsed on Anna's arm the first time we met, I went out to where she stood, just beyond the light from the house. As she smoked, she was holding onto herself, as if trying not to shake. She'd been crying.

'Was I rude?' she said. 'I can't tell sometimes.'

'Siobhan's drunk. She'll have forgotten all about it in the morning.'

'I didn't want to spoil it.'

'Spoil what?'

I heard David's voice from the house. Then laughter, and Siobhan shrieking the way she does.

'How did she upset you?'

'She thinks what to paint is the least of it,' said Anna.

'She always says the first thing that comes into her head. She's such an idiot sometimes.'

'It sounds romantic, doesn't it, being an artist in Berlin? I was very excited, fresh out of college, full of myself. But when it came to it, I simply couldn't paint. The truth is, I didn't actually know what to paint. Now, what good is that?'

'What did you do?'

'I'd like to say I'm not really sure. But it's not true. I started drinking, and drugs were easy to find in Prenzlauer Berg, I can tell you. And I did other things, things I remember all too well...'

As her words trailed off, I imagined her lying on a dirty studio floor in front of a blank canvas. The image was too vivid in my mind; I saw the blood pouring from her arm.

'What happened?' I said.

'I saw what I had to paint,' she said, drawing on her cigarette.

'You had visions? Like Bernadette?'

'If only.' She exhaled the smoke and watched it rise up into the air. 'I just had to give in to something. Something I was frightened of.'

'Lucy says you're a shaman. Is it something like that?'

'Like a witch?' she said. 'That should put you off.'

'I just think you're very talented.'

'I have a talent for spoiling things. I know that much.'

'You haven't spoilt anything.'

'You're very kind, Verity.'

'Come on,' I said, putting my arm around her. 'There's something very special for dessert. I made it just for you.'

We walked back into the house. Anna, her face still streaked with tears, apologised to Siobhan, who was so relieved, and quite drunk, she stood up and embraced her. I went into the kitchen to fetch the caramel chocolate tart. As I set it down in the centre of the table, David was telling one of his long drawn-out stories. I'd heard him tell it too many times before, and I just laughed when the others did. In truth, I'd stopped listening.

*

Parties, dinners, outings to restaurants and gallery openings; I couldn't be bothered to go unless I knew Anna would be there. We went shopping together. I was with her the day she bought a bright plastic watch, and when I said I liked it, she insisted on buying one for me. It was bright orange. I often wore it instead of the Rolex David had given me for my fiftieth last year. It seemed more fun, less bourgeois. Siobhan disapproved. 'It's too young for you,' she said.

Anna had bought a house. Not in a great area, mind you, but a solid Victorian terrace all the same. She'd painted all the rooms white and made everything so minimal and clean. Except for her studio. That was an absolute mess, with odd little tables covered in jars, brushes and squashed up tubes of paint, which had dripped down onto the bare floorboards. Paintings, finished and half-finished, were leaning against the wall and there was always one, an absolutely fabulous one, in progress on the easel. I visited as often as I could. The room reeked; a heady aroma of turps and oils and cigarette smoke I found irresistible.

One day, I was sitting in what Anna called 'the clean chair' ('so you don't get paint on your lovely clothes') and she was lying back on an old Ikea recliner, wearing a navy boiler suit covered in spatters of paint. She had been on edge ever since I'd arrived; I was going to finish the coffee she'd made me, and leave. She lit another cigarette.

'Don't you ever feel like just letting go?' she said, staring up at the ceiling as she exhaled.

'Whatever do you mean?'

'You know, like forgetting your manners and just letting yourself come out. Your true self. Even if it wasn't nice. At least it would be the real you.'

'Like Mrs Hyde?' I said, trying to make her laugh, but she just shrugged her shoulders.

'Who's the real you, Verity?'

'What's the matter?'

'I get bored. I'm sick of being a good girl.'

'A good girl?'

'This painting is fucking awful,' she said, getting up and standing in front of the easel.

'Perhaps you just need a break.'

I went and stood next to her.

'What do you know?' she said, turning to face me.

She picked up a Stanley knife from the table, slid out the blade and raised it up to cut into the canvas. I grabbed her wrist and held it fast, so she couldn't move.

'Don't. It'll be as bad as cutting yourself.'

'I don't care.'

I forced her hand down to point the blade at the floor.

'Do you want to hurt me too?' I said.

'No. And anyway, you're too strong.'

'Pilates and regular weight training. I'm a bourgeois cliché, Anna.'

'That's not who you are,' she said, and released her grip. The knife dropped to the floor. 'Don't go, Verity. You've wanted to leave ever since you got here. I could tell.'

'So, it's my fault?'

'No. I told you I always spoil things. The things I care about.'

*

After I bought the painting Anna wanted to celebrate by having a dinner party. Oh, and would I help her because I was such a good cook, and she would really like it if we could make 'that mushroom dish we had at your house.' Of course, I was pleased she wanted my help, and we planned the menu together.

I picked her up on the morning of the dinner party to take her mushroom picking, driving out of the city in the Range Rover, up into the shire where we could roam from pasture to woodland and across the fields again.

The leaves had turned all across the valley, and there was a chill in the early morning air. We picked field mushrooms, chanterelles from the woods, and some Caesar's mushrooms. A good crop, I thought, and quite enough for the dinner party. But I wanted to find some Fairy Ring Champignon and led the way across some open pasture to where I'd found them before.

I'd taken the field guide with us to help identify poisonous mushrooms. Well, I knew it pretty well, but Anna said she wanted to learn. She was holding the book open, looking at it as she walked, but she was like a teenager, nervy and unfocused. She walked listlessly behind me, and I had to wait for her to me catch up.

'What about magic mushrooms?' she said. 'Imagine everyone seeing things that weren't there. It would be doing them a favour. People like Siobhan. It would awaken her creative side. She'd see something outside her cosy little world then, wouldn't she?'

'That's a bit rich, isn't it?'

'Well,' she said. 'I'd really like to see things that weren't there. Wouldn't you?'

'You're joking.'

'Am I? Liberty Caps are what we want. Magic mushrooms.'

I realised she knew what they looked like; she'd always known. She moved quickly away from me.

'Shrooms,' she called out, pointing down at the corner of the field.

That's what kids call them, I thought, as she stooped down.

'Why are you picking them?'

'Oh, don't worry. They're just for me.'

'Is this for your visions?'

'No, of course not,' she said, stretching her arm out and opening her hand, to let me see the little mushrooms falling to the ground. I thought she was in a strop, but she came and held onto my arm and looked into the basket. 'Are there enough now?'

I laughed, glad because her mood seemed to have changed, and we walked back down the valley slope to where the car was parked.

'You think I need to grow up, don't you?' said Anna, as we drove back towards the main road under a canopy of trees, bright with autumn colours.

'Don't be silly.'

'You don't trust me, do you?'

'What makes you say that?'

'Let me take the wheel,' she said, touching my sleeve.

'What for?'

'You know what for.' She reached over and gripped the steering wheel. 'Let go.'

I lifted my hands up. She was right, I did know; I felt a tremor in my stomach. A rush of feeling made me catch my breath. I stopped looking at the road ahead, and turned to Anna instead, letting my eye trace her profile, the sharp angle of her nose. Pushing my foot down on the accelerator, I enjoyed the feeling of the engine pulling hard, and watched her smile. I checked the rear-view mirror. Bright yellow leaves flew up from the road behind us, and danced in the slipstream of the car.

Back at her house we worked together in the kitchen, but by about three o'clock Anna leaned against the worktop, and started watching me, a bored look on her face. It could have been my fault, I suppose. I have a tendency to take over, because I know the proper way to do things.

I didn't see what time it was when she started on the gin, she was never apologetic about her drinking, but it didn't help her mood. She had an edge to her, like the one she'd had earlier in the day. I tried to show how angry she made me by banging and bustling around the kitchen.

'I hope I'm not in the way, Verity.' She said it softly and before I could answer, she'd just slipped out of the room.

There was a tension in the air, but I couldn't think how to make sense of it.

I was relieved when I had to go home to change, even though there was still a lot to do. The table had to be laid with candles and things. To be honest, she had become quite untidy in recent weeks and the chaos of her studio was spilling out into the rest of the house.

David and I arrived early. I thought I would have to help with the finishing touches, but there was no need. Anna had laid the table with a red Damask cloth and set candles all around the dining room so it was quite magical. She wore a vintage Biba gown, and she looked delightful.

'I'm sorry,' she said. 'Have I been an awful pain?' There were tears in her eyes. 'I couldn't bear it if we fell out.'

David carried a case of wine in from the taxi, and we had a drink together. Anna had already put the mushrooms in the oven and before the others were due to arrive, I went to check on them. It was then I saw a Liberty Cap mushroom on the worktop next to the cooker. I took the dish from the oven and searched it anxiously, turning everything over with a slotted spoon, but I couldn't be sure if she had, in some malicious fit, mixed some 'shrooms' into the dish. I put it back in the oven. To be honest, I really didn't know what else to do.

The doorbell rang, an irritating buzz like a demented wasp, and I heard Siobhan's voice.

'Oh what a lovely dress, Anna. Is it vintage? I wish I could carry off lovely old clothes like that, but I never think to look in charity shops.'

It made me think about what Anna had said about Siobhan. Something about awakening her creative side with magic mushrooms. *She'd see something outside her cosy little world then, wouldn't she?* Could Anna do such a thing? Was this another test, like the thing in the car this afternoon?

Lucy and Mark arrived, they had brought Catherine, and as everyone fussed about and David organised the drinks, I realised we were the same group who had been at my house the night Anna had come for dinner. Now, she kept looking at me as we had our aperitifs in the sitting room, giving me odd little looks, either apologetic or mischievous, I couldn't tell.

'It's time to go through,' said Anna, with a musical, almost sarcastic, lilt to her voice. 'Time for Verity's fantastic wild mushrooms. We went out and collected them this morning. But don't worry. Verity made sure we didn't pick any dodgy ones.'

As everyone started to move, I made a decision and rushed into the kitchen.

'Let me help, Anna,' I said. 'I'll get them out.'

Before she could object, or try and stop me, I'd put the oven glove on my right hand and pulled the dish out of the oven. But I deliberately grabbed it with my left hand, as if I needed to balance it. The heat seared my skin. I screamed and let go. Something shattered and I looked down. On the kitchen floor, amongst shards of broken crockery, the *cèpes à la génoise* lay in a pool of oil.

Everyone was fussing around me. I held up my hand for Anna to see the red weals beginning to form on my palm and fingers. I wanted to say, look what you've made me do, as she rushed over to me shouting 'Verity! Verity!' She came so very close I could smell her, and she gently held my hand, kissing it as a mother might. In the cloud of panic swirling around us, a tap running, Siobhan taking control, it seemed we were together in a way invisible to the others. Anna looked into my eyes and gave me a smile I knew was just for me, and I smiled back.

*

Anna has gone back to Berlin to sort out some 'unfinished business', but she has promised to come back to me in the spring. I come into this room on these winter afternoons, when the house has a quiet deserted feel and dull grey daylight struggles to fill even this small space. I sit on the plain wooden chair and gaze at the painting, which completely fills my field of vision.

It is a picture of a naked woman, sullen and defiant, her pale legs open towards the viewer. Rising up from her vulva, or descending down into it, is a swirling vortex, a mass of red, black and brown pigment, so ragged and half wrought it might be a mixture of blood and excrement. Caught in this maelstrom are innumerable small creatures. Some are recognisable; hares, badgers, mice, and toads. But others are strange mutations, bizarre assemblages of fur, teeth and scales.

Being in front of the painting is like being in a dream, and I am pulled into it, falling with these creatures tumbling all around me. They are wide-eyed and open-mouthed, whether in ecstasy or terror, it is difficult to know.

Before and After

Every day was like this. It was after ten o'clock in the morning and I still hadn't opened the lounge curtains. Couldn't be bothered. I was sitting on the sofa in my dressing gown eating a bowl of Special K. Of course, I knew it wouldn't do any good; it wasn't part of a calorie-controlled diet. Dave just pretends there's nothing wrong. Perhaps he can't see the signs. Or doesn't want to.

Milk was running down my chin and I just kept looking at the television.

Kelly Costa was on The Morning Show. She was talking about how she had been in her own private hell. How she had been comfort eating and drinking and using cocaine. She'd become a sex addict, she said, and it was all because she hated herself. They showed that clip of her when she was crying and really drunk on a TV chat show. Then a photo of her on a beach, the one that was in all the gossip mags last year. Boy, did she look a state back then, all puffy-eyed and really chubby. Fat and Ugly. And I remember thinking, I'm not so bad, not so bad as someone famous.

But now she'd gone and lost loads of weight and toned up. She looked really good, and when she stood up to show off her new figure, the audience clapped and cheered. She smiled and showed her lovely white teeth and said she'd got back her self-respect, and was in a loving relationship with a man who loves her for who she really is. Now she just wants to make up for all the bad stuff and make a good home for her kids, who, she has realised, are the most important things in her life. That's how I feel about Tara. I super-love her because I'm her mother and a mother's love is just something you can't help. Like being hungry in front of a big chocolate cake.

Tara came in and leaned against the doorframe in that lazy way she has, holding her mobile phone. She is heavier than I was at her age, her plump tummy and midriff spilling over the top of her low-cut jeans.

'Watching daytime telly, then?' she said, looking down at her phone, stroking her thumb over the screen, always somewhere else.

'Yes,' I said, turning back to the television.

She came and sat on the arm of the sofa.

'Omigod. Is that really Kelly Costa? She looks amazing.'

'Doesn't she?' I said.

I wanted to reach for her hand, but I was worried she would pull it away.

'This is such a bad habit,' she said, and jumped up.

But then she kissed me on the cheek. It was then I knew what I had to do. 'Thank you, Kelly Costa,' I said to myself. Thank you for showing me there is a way out. When I heard Tara slam the front door, I went into the kitchen and took another one of my pills; I needed all the help I could get. I was going to change my life. I would diet. I would exercise. I would learn to love myself.

What I needed was a before photograph. It is only in a photograph of yourself that you can see what you truly are. That's what I believe, and I know it is what Kelly Costa believes. Those pictures from last year's holiday with me pale and pink, hiding under a beach umbrella. I would get them out now, I thought, and confront myself with the worst of it.

An older black photograph album was pushed in between the others I keep on the shelf unit in the spare room. It was amongst the things they had given me at the nursing home. I don't know why, but I took it downstairs with the rest. And after I put them all on the dining room table, it was the one I looked at first. Funny thing was, I'd never wanted to look at it before, to see all those pictures of me with Mum, never with Dad. Perhaps there was nothing wrong with that. After all, he was always the one with the camera, wasn't he?

What was there to be frightened of? There was a nice picture of me in my Girl Guide uniform on a camping trip, and a photo taken for the local paper when I passed my Cycling Proficiency Test, with the cutting pasted on the opposite page, and another one from a school prize day. Mum must have been really proud of that one because she'd had a copy framed.

A small square colour photograph slipped onto the table as I turned the pages. It took me by surprise. Of course, I knew it was a picture of me, but there was something different about it. Something different about me. I was leaning against the trunk of a large tree, wearing a pretty green dress and Clarks sandals with white ankle socks. My hair was in pigtails and it was before I started to wear glasses. I must have been about ten or eleven years old. I looked happy.

And I remembered everything, all at once. The tree was an oak. It was outside the village school, and there was a boy with a camera.

His name was Carl. He had dark hair and blue eyes, and long curling eyelashes. They were like the eyes of a doll. He lived on the council estate and Susan had said he was a Gypsy. All through junior school he had been just another boy in my class. But in our last year I would find myself talking to him in the playground. He knew all about wild animals and the names of all the birds. Susan and the others used to say, oh look at Ruth, she has a boyfriend. But I did not mind at all because I liked him.

Carl started waiting for me by the school gates and he would walk me home, back to the village through the wood. One day, he said there was a secret place he wanted to show me. We went off the main path and there, hidden from the world, was a little hut with earth walls and a roof of corrugated iron. There was a small wooden door with proper hinges. He crouched down and crawled in and I followed him.

There was brown lino on the floor and two old car seats made of leather, and an old radio with lots of wires coming off it. One went into something like a vase with a lid on the top of it, and the others went off into jars and tin cans all over the floor.

'What's all this for?' I asked.

'I'm building a Time Machine.'

Well, of course I said I didn't believe him.

'I saw a film about it. At the Essoldo. It was called The Time Machine. The other people in the film didn't believe the man either. But it was true. He went into the future. The world had gone bad so he went to make it better.'

'It just looks like some old junk.'

'This,' he said, tapping the radio, 'takes all the past that's here, in all these old things I've found,' he pointed to the jars and cans, 'and turns it into a magic power, which will let me travel through time.'

He showed me the things in the jars and tins. Bullets he said were from the war, some old farthings and silver sixpences, medals and bits of an old magazine. In one of the jars, all on its own, was a Roman coin, and in another a flint arrowhead with the skull of a rabbit.

'What's that vase thing?'

'It's called an urn, and it has my Grandad's ashes in. He was cremated, which means burnt. He was very old and some of his soul is still in there.'

'Make it work then.'

'It isn't finished yet. I need to get some electricity. Then, when I switch it on, I'll be able to go into the future.'

'Come here,' I said, lying down.

He came and lay beside me. He kissed me, which is what I'd wanted him to do. And then we went home.

The next day he was carrying a brown canvas case and inside was a camera the colour of dark chocolate. A Brownie 127, I think.

'You look nice today,' he said. 'I'll be able to take a good photograph because it's sunny.'

I went and leant against the big oak tree opposite the school. I was smiling, not just because I was having my photograph taken, but because I was happy.

'It'll be in colour,' he said, and clicked the camera.

We went to the little hut again and I saw he had made a circle of all of the jars around one of the car seats, and there was a big battery, the kind farmers used for electric fences. All around the inside he had put up lines of string and used clothes pegs to hang up photographs. Lots of them. Some of them looked really old.

'The Time Machine is nearly finished,' he said.

But I wasn't interested. I lay down because I wanted him to kiss me. So he came and kissed me, and then he kissed me some more. I liked it, but strange feelings came over me and I was worried we would get into trouble about it, and said I had to get home.

I started to avoid Carl then, because I knew I would want to go to the hut with him, but I didn't dare. After school I started walking home with Susan and some of the other girls, and let them tease me about falling out with my 'boyfriend' so we would be friends again.

In the summer I was waiting to go to the Grammar School. I had passed my Eleven Plus and my Mum and Dad were really pleased. We were going to go up to Scotland on holiday, and it felt as if everything was going to be new. One day, just before we went, it was after tea, I heard a knock at the door and Mum went to see who it was.

'It's that boy from your school,' she said. 'The one who lives on the estate.'

I went to the door and was really pleased to see Carl standing on the step.

'I have brought the photo I took of you,' he said, taking it out of a yellow packet and handing it to me.

'Do you like it?'

'Yes,' I said, and I called my Mum to show her.

'Oh, it's really lovely,' she said. 'Did you take it?'

He nodded and said, 'Ruth can keep it if she wants it.'

'Can I pay you for it?'

'No,' he said. 'It's a present for Ruth.'

I wanted to go to the hut in the woods with him, even though he wouldn't meet my eyes. I turned to Mum anyway, and said we were going out to play.

'Let's go to your hut,' I said, and when we were in the woods, I held his hand. Even though I could tell there was something wrong, all I could do when we got to the hut was to lie down and try to pull him on top of me. I wanted him to kiss me again, but he shook off my hand.

'I've finished the Time Machine.'

'Don't be stupid,' I said, looking around at all the photographs of people he had hung up. There were even more than before and I thought they were all looking at me.

'It worked. I went into the future, and you were standing out there.' He pointed out through the open door, into the wood. 'You were old, like your Mum and I knew it was you. You looked really sad.' And he started crying.

'You're just making it up,' I said.

I was angry because he was crying and I didn't understand why he was saying those things. It was as if he wanted to make me unhappy. He kept talking about the Time Machine, which made me think he was mad. I ran home through the wood. Branches caught against my hair and clothes, brambles scratched my legs and when I got home, I stumbled, crying, in through the kitchen door.

'What a state you're in, Ruth,' Mum said when she saw me. 'What's happened?'

I didn't say anything.

'What has that boy done to you?' she asked.

But I just went up to my room and lay on the bed.

Later, Dad came up and said, 'What's this about a boy, Ruth?'

I could tell he was angry about it, because he was hard and cold. I felt ashamed of something, but I didn't understand why, and I started to cry again.

The police came to the house. There were two of them, a plainclothes detective and a uniformed policewoman. They sat in the living room with me while Mum and Dad waited in the kitchen.

The policewoman was really nice and friendly, all smiles and sparkling eyes. She asked me about school and what I liked doing.

Then, was Carl my friend? And what did we do together? So I told them about the little hut in the woods.

'Did he touch you, Ruth?' said the detective.

The question frightened me. It was like a hole in the ground I might fall into. I had wanted Carl to kiss me more than anything else. Perhaps I had wanted him to touch me as well.

Then I said out loud what Carl had said about the Time Machine and seeing me when I was older. About how angry I was because he'd said I was going to be sad when I was grown up.

The detective went out into the hall and spoke to Mum and Dad. He had left the door open a little, and I could hear them talking. There were words like *highly-strung* and *police time*. The policewoman just sat on the sofa watching me, no smile, no longer nice and friendly.

Dad was angry, but he didn't say anything. Mum sent me to bed early, to get some rest, she said. I lay down and heard them talking downstairs, their voices going backwards and forwards, on and on, until I fell asleep.

We ended up going on holiday early, up to Fort William, which is where we always went. Dad only stayed for a week, but Mum and I stayed for nearly the whole summer. When September came, I didn't go to the Grammar School. Dad had got me into a boarding school instead. They sold the house in the village and moved to the city. I never saw Carl again. Nor Susan, nor any of them.

*

I found the photographs from last year's holiday. There was the one of me on the beach in a black one-piece and an awkward smile, which Dave had insisted on taking. Even the scarf I'd tied around my waist couldn't hide the awful truth. I held the picture in one hand, the one Carl had taken in the other, and looked at them side by side. It was not just the difference in age or weight.

It was in the way I held myself, the way my girl smile flowed out of the photograph.

Now it was all gone, I thought. I was happy then and now something was wrong with me. I saw myself from above, an overweight middle-aged woman, in a grubby pink dressing gown, sobbing so hard she thinks her chest will burst. When crying is over there is always a sense of calm because all the feeling has spilled out of you. I got dressed and tidied the photographs away.

When Dave came home, I was sitting in the kitchen drinking tea.

'Had a good day?' he said, turning on the tap to fill the kettle. I listened to the water rushing into it.

'I was looking at some old photographs, from when I was a girl.'

'Lovely,' he said. 'You can show me later.'

I didn't say any more about it, and he didn't ask. But I was glad he didn't say anything about the cakes, the packet of biscuits and the bars of chocolate in the kitchen bin. It's difficult enough to change, but if you tell people you're going to try, well you're just setting yourself up to fail, aren't you? That's my experience, anyway.

As usual, I couldn't sleep. The thought of the photograph, the image of it just went around and around in my head. I kept hearing Carl's voice, 'You were old like your Mum…You looked really sad.' There was no sense in any of it, except that his prophecy had come true.

At about five o'clock I slipped out of bed and took my Amitriptyline. After showering, I dried my hair with a towel so I didn't wake Dave with the hair drier, and dressed in jeans and a fleecy. I had a breakfast of tea without milk, and toast with a thin scraping of low-fat spread. Quiet as a mouse, I got out the half bottle of vodka I keep in my knickers drawer for emergencies, put an anorak in the boot of the car in case it rained, and drove to the Esso garage to fill up. The picture Carl had taken of me was in my handbag. The sky above the A1 was overcast, but the Amitriptyline filled me with a fuzzy warmth.

I came off the motorway at the right junction, and although I recognised the roads, there was something odd about them. When I got to the village, I parked across the road from the house we used to live in, but it didn't look the way I remembered it. It was as if it wasn't anything to do with me anymore, as if I had never been here in my life. I started to cry and couldn't catch my breath.

I had to work out how to drive to the school and I was not driving very well, probably because I had taken more Amitriptyline, chasing the pills down with the vodka, which I know you shouldn't do. I got there eventually and parked the car, bumping one of the front wheels onto the kerb. Again, nothing looked quite right. It was as if they had taken the old school down and tried to rebuild it so it looked the same, but it hadn't worked because they'd made it smaller. It was deserted as if all the children had gone away. A dull light fell from the grey sky, through the windows and into the classrooms where I had once been a child, a cruel light that showed how empty everything had become.

The oak tree was still there, and I followed the path into the woods. I came to the stream we used to have to cross on stepping-stones. There was a little bridge there now, and I came off the path, searching in the undergrowth for rusty bits of corrugated iron, the remains of the earth walls, something to show where the hut had been.

I must have fainted because I was lying on the ground, amongst the brambles and the nettles, the smell of damp earth in my nostrils. Stones and twigs were pressing against my cheek, but I couldn't be bothered to move. I closed my eyes and thought of Carl, sitting in one of the old car seats, with the radio, the jars and the photographs all around him. He knew I would come here today. If I stayed like this, and just listened to the leaves rustling in the wind, he would come and lie down beside me. He would kiss me just as he had done before, but this time I would not be afraid.

Spitfire

Eventually I started to get tired of waiting for my Dad to come out. I didn't know whose house it was, but I knew he was in there. I was on what Mum called one of my wanderings and I'd seen his bike chained to the drainpipe by the side door. I'd recognised it by the way the white tape was wrapped around the drop handlebars. Really neat, because that's the way he did things.

I stood for a bit thinking he should be coming out, because it was nearly time for tea, and Mum didn't like it if we were late. In the end I went through the gate and had a look in the front window because there was a light on. There was no one there, so I went round the back and peeked in through the kitchen window.

A woman was bent over the table with her dress up at the back. Dad had hold of her by the waist and it looked like his trousers were falling down. But he didn't seem to care because he was rocking backwards and forwards with his eyes closed. And the woman was moaning really loud. I wasn't too young not to know what was happening. The blood rushed to my face and I ran home. I didn't know what else to do.

THIRTEEN

Mum was in a bit of a state because Dad hadn't come home, and we sat at the kitchen table eating our tea. It was bangers and mash with baked beans, which was one of my favourites. Mum didn't touch hers. She didn't say anything and just stared at Dad's place on the other side of the table, and I couldn't help thinking it was just like the table in the woman's house. Blue Formica with steel legs.

After I'd finished my tea, Mum told me to go and watch the telly. But I couldn't really concentrate because she was in a bad mood, and I thought she was angry with me although I hadn't done anything. I was glad when I heard Dad's footsteps on the path, that sound he made when he walked, a scuff with every third step as he wheeled his bike to the shed. Now he was home I thought everything would be alright, but Mum started at him as soon as he was through the kitchen door. She started swearing, using words like 'fuck' and 'whore'. Things like that. Then she must have started throwing things at him, because it sounded like plates or glasses smashing.

I went through because I wanted them to stop. But I was in my socks and trod on something sharp, which really hurt my foot, and I couldn't walk properly and fell down. But even though I was in pain and there was blood everywhere and I was begging them to stop, Mum just went on and on.

Dad told her to calm down. 'Think about the boy,' he said, by which he meant me. But she wouldn't stop shouting and said she would cut his cock off. And I was still asking her to stop and saying look at the blood coming out of my foot.

Dad got me up to the bathroom and I sat on the toilet while he used some tweezers to pull bits of glass out of my foot. He washed it and put on some TCP, which stung, and then a pad of cotton wool with a plaster. He said that I didn't have to go to school tomorrow, that I could take the day off.

'I saw you with that woman,' I said.

'What woman? What are you talking about?'

I told him about seeing his bike and how I'd waited for him to come out and then how I'd gone round the back to see where he was.

'I looked through the window. I saw you with that woman. I saw what you were doing.'

'I think you've made a mistake, son,' he said. 'Bikes like mine are ten a penny. I wasn't with any woman. I was down the pub. That's why your Mum's upset. She doesn't like me going down the pub. It wasn't me you saw. Okay?'

I nodded, like I agreed with him, because I wanted to believe him. I wanted everything to be okay and anyway, I didn't mind having a day off school. But his breath didn't smell of beer like it did when he'd been down the pub.

The next day, when he came home from work, Dad brought me a model aircraft kit, a Spitfire I had been saving up for, saying this is another one for your collection. He bought Mum a present too, a necklace she'd had her eye on. That wasn't all. He said he was going to take us to Butlin's, the one at Filey, for a week in the summer.

Mum cheered up a lot after that, and when we were all in front of the telly on Friday night, she and Dad sat on the sofa together. He put his arm around her and they held hands. I built the Spitfire that weekend, really taking care over it, and painting it up properly. When I showed Dad, he said what a good job I'd made of it. That it was just like the real thing. I didn't hang it from the ceiling like the other models I'd made, I put it on a stand on my desk so I could look at it when I did my homework.

We went to Butlin's by train, and even had to change trains, which was pretty exciting what with the guards' whistles and the announcements and everything. I knew then I was going to have a great holiday. There was a boating lake where I went nearly all the time, rowing myself around. Mum and Dad went to the swimming pool nearly every day, and at night they went out dancing.

We were staying in what they called a chalet. There were two bedrooms, but the walls were thin and I heard Mum giggling at night, and sometimes they were moaning a bit. I started to think about seeing Dad with the woman, but when I heard Mum call out, 'I love you, Frank,' I knew I'd made a mistake. That it wasn't him I'd seen, even though the bike looked just like his.

I met a girl at the boating lake and I rowed her around in a dinghy. She let me kiss her and we went around the back of the boathouse and lay on the grass and kissed for ages. She bit me on the neck, making a big red mark and Mum made a fuss about it, asking me what I was coming to.

Dad thought it was funny. 'It's a love-bite, Martha,' he said. 'The boy's in love.'

He started laughing and so did Mum. The girl was called Avril and we went around together for the rest of the week. I told her that I loved her and she said I was sweet, but that there was no future in it. 'It's just a holiday romance,' she said. But she still let me lie on top of her and kiss her.

Mum was so happy after that week and when we got back, she wasn't in a bad mood all the time. She stopped taking those tablets she got from the doctor. Valium they were called, and Dad said they were the cause of all the trouble we'd been having.

When I went back to school things were better than before. I got on with people better. Martin Jackson stopped being so funny with me and I told him that I'd met this girl on holiday and that I'd done it with her, even though it wasn't true.

I started going round to his house. It was a big house with a big lawn at the back with trees and bushes. His dad had given him an air rifle, a BSA Meteor with a telescopic sight, and we used to shoot at old tin cans down at the bottom of the garden.

When I met his mum and dad, his mum asked me where my people were from, and I said my Dad was from Southampton. She said that was nice and Martin said I'd been to Butlin's for my summer holiday. She said they always went to France because they had a house there, and Martin's dad laughed and asked me what I'd got up to at Butlin's, because he'd heard stories about the girls there. I told him about the boating lake and how I'd rowed around in a dinghy. He said they had a boat, a sailing boat, and if I liked messing about on boats so much, he would take 'you boys' up for a day's sailing.

When I got home, I asked Mum what it meant when someone asked where your people were from. She said they were trying to find out your social standing. I didn't really understand, but Dad said it was a cheeky question and wanted to know who was asking.

I told him it was Martin's mum and he asked me what she was like. I said she was a bit posh, but Mr Jackson was nice and he was going to take me and Martin sailing. Dad said it was alright for some.

The next weekend Martin's dad took us up to a marina in Northumberland. They let me row the dinghy from the shore to the sailing boat. It was like being on the boating lake at Butlin's, only better, and Mr Jackson said I was a natural, and when we went out to sea, me and Martin worked the sails and the ropes and I just thought it was amazing.

Mum said it was good for me to have made a new friend at school, because sometimes scholarship boys were looked down on. I told Martin about the Spitfire and he showed me a load of the model aircraft he'd made. But he hadn't made them very well. There was glue everywhere and the decals were all skewed, and he hadn't even bothered to paint them. He said we should hang them from the clothes line and shoot at them with his air rifle.

It was getting near Bonfire Night and I said I would come on Saturday afternoon, and that I would go and buy some bangers on the way so we could blow some of them up. He thought that was a great idea, and said that because his mum and dad would be out, he would show me some of his dad's dirty magazines and we could look at them together.

That Saturday Mum and I had beans on toast together. Dad had gone off on his bike because he said he had to go and see a man about a dog. Mum thought that was funny, but she said it meant he was going to the pub with one of his mates. But she didn't mind because he worked hard all week to give us a nice life, and he needed to let off steam.

I decided to take the Spitfire to show off to Martin. I emptied my toy soldiers out of a shoebox, and put the Spitfire in with some crumpled newspaper to stop it from getting broken.

When I went downstairs Mum had her friend round, a woman called Stella who always winked at me when she caught me looking at her cleavage, as if she knew what I was thinking.

'We're drinking gin,' said Stella. 'While your Dad's down the pub.'

'What's good for the goose,' said Mum, and they both laughed at that.

When I kissed Mum goodbye, Stella said, 'Don't I get one?' and I had to kiss her on the cheek and she smelled of cigarettes and perfume.

I went to the newsagents and bought a box of six bangers to take to Martin's. I took a shortcut to his house along that street, the one where I thought I'd seen my Dad's bike outside that house. I felt funny about it, because it felt as if I was going back in time. But it wasn't funny ha-ha. It was funny peculiar because when I passed the house and looked, there was the bike chained to the drainpipe, the way it had been before. And I knew it was my Dad's bike, because of the way the white tape was wrapped around the handlebars, and then I knew he'd lied. To me and Mum. That everything was a lie.

Martin was surprised when I showed him the Spitfire. He said it was really good, just like the real thing, which is what Dad had said. I said I wanted to tie it up on the line and shoot at it with his air rifle. Or tie a banger to it, I didn't mind.

'But it's too good for that, isn't it?' he said. 'I mean, are you sure? Didn't your Dad buy it for you?'

He put his arm around my shoulder, as if he knew something was wrong. I wanted to cry, to tell him what had happened. To tell him how scared I was.

'It's kid's stuff,' I said. 'Let's just have a bit of fun.'

I tied the Spitfire up to the clothes line, so that it was hanging there as if it was flying. Martin hung up a model of a German plane he'd made, and we decided to take turns shooting at them. He shot at his first and missed.

I took the air rifle off him and broke the barrel to put the pellet in, and snapped it shut. I pulled the butt tight into my shoulder, and squinted with one eye through the telescopic sight, aiming at the Spitfire. I was shaking and Martin asked me if I was alright. I told him there was nothing wrong. But I gritted my teeth and closed both my eyes. I thought how much I hated him for having an air rifle, and a posh mum who looked like a model, and his dad and her for having a big house and a fancy car and a boat on a marina. Because it was nothing to them.

And because he wanted me to look at his dad's dirty magazines with him.

Afterwards we went up to his room. He had a bottle of his dad's whisky and poured some into two heavy glasses. It tasted horrible, but Martin said it would make me feel better, and it was best to drink it down in one go. It burned my throat and we had some more, and I started to feel funny. Then we sat on the bed and looked at his dad's dirty magazines, at the pictures of women with no clothes on.

The feelings I had then made me think about Avril, the girl at the boating lake and everything we'd done together. And I remembered Dad with that woman, what he was doing to her when she was bent over that kitchen table, the one that looked just like the one in our house. The same colour and everything.

I got up and went over to the window and looked down to the bottom of the garden. I felt dizzy. Martin said to come and sit back on the bed with him. He said it in a whiney voice, the way Stella had asked for a kiss, and I knew I would. But I wanted to see the Spitfire. It was all smashed up, and what was left of it was hanging from the line like a broken bird.

The Red Canoe

What do you say to a dying man?

Brian sipped his coffee and tried to remember what barbers talked about. They asked you where you were going on holiday, or who you thought would win the match on Saturday. Things that were going to happen. But you can't talk about the future to a dying man, can you?

He washed his mug in the kitchen sink, and looked out of the window at the back of his brother's house. It had been his parents' house, the family home. Brian had lived there until he left to join the army. But Dennis had never left. He'd stayed put, taking over the tenancy after Mam died. The old council house, the render dirty with soot and weather, was an exact copy of the house Brian lived in now. Maybe that was why he'd bought it when Maggie Thatcher made all the councils sell off their houses for nothing. He would have been stupid not to take advantage of a thing like that.

Now, none of the houses on the estate was owned by the council. Those that were still rented, like Dennis's, had been given over to a property management company. Nothing was the same as it used to be. But what good did fretting about it do?

THIRTEEN

Dennis had been ill, something to do with fluid on his lungs. And then they found out he had cancer. Just like that. Pat, his eldest sister, told Brian the diagnosis had come too late, and that Dennis was going to die. Brian should go and see him, is what she meant. Before it was too late.

He hadn't seen his brother for a long time. Not since Pat had been running him to hospital once a week, to have the fluid drained from his lungs. Brian couldn't face a sick room. Not since their parents died.

But he didn't really have an excuse. All he had to do was to walk down to the bottom of his garden and step over the fence. Today, he stopped to look at the state of Dennis's vegetable patch. He should have helped out. Kept on top of the weeds, at least, he thought as he went on up to the house. He still had a key. But the side door was open, and he stepped into the dim lobby they used to call the back kitchen.

Here was the fridge, and the electric cooker Mam used in the summer to save firing up the Rayburn. Something caught Brian unawares. A musty smell. Not of stale cooking, but of the sweat trapped in the coats and jackets hanging on the wall. It was the smell of his father.

The main kitchen ran the length of the house. Dennis had bought himself a new widescreen television and put it where the old TV had been. But everything else was the same. The table, where his mother had served her famous Sunday teas, and the chairs with their worn leather cushions. And the big chest of drawers and, on top of it, the cupboard with glass doors. Over the years, postcards and family photographs had been tucked between the frame and the glass. Inside were the best cups and saucers and the fancy glasses, and odd souvenirs from holidays in Blackpool or Scarborough.

Brian shouted out a hello. Pat called down and told him to come up. He went through into the cramped sitting room. Here was more familiar furniture; a sideboard, a three-piece suite and a coffee table. But now he had to thread his way between the stacks of newspapers and magazines Dennis had taken to collecting.

At the top of the stairs he stopped to catch his breath and heard his sisters' voices. Chattering away about nothing, as usual. Across the landing the door of the small back bedroom was open. It had been his room before he left home, and the narrow bed was made up as if someone still slept there.

On the wall above the bed was a framed colour photograph of a lake surrounded by snow covered mountains. And on the lake was a red canoe. Brian stood in the doorway, looking at the picture, until Pat called out. Asking him if he'd got lost.

'I'm here,' he said, and went into his brother's room.

Dennis was in the same bedroom he'd always slept in, the one Brian had shared with him and Stan, until Pat and Jean left home. There was only one bed in the room now, and Dennis was lying there, propped up against a pile of pillows, the covers pulled back and his pyjama top undone. He was hot, he said. Fucking hot was how he put it, and the window was open to let the breeze in. Dennis's old white belly was pushed out and his eyes stared at something. Brian remembered when they were boys, the time Dennis got stuck up a tree and couldn't get down. His eyes had been like that then, because he'd been too scared to jump.

His sisters, Pat and Jean, sat next to the bed, side by side on odd chairs. They were going on about an old calendar on the wall, open at a picture of Marilyn Monroe, because it was what Dennis appeared to be looking at. They were asking him if he liked her, liked her best of all the movie stars, and without waiting for an answer they went on about how beautiful she was. How they didn't make them like that anymore.

Brian was glad of his sisters' chatter. To avoid looking at his brother he walked over to the calendar and took it off the wall. The picture was of Marilyn in a gold dress that showed off the full shape of her breasts. The thing was over thirty years old. Dennis, he realised, had had it open at the same page, the page for June, for all that time. The picture had faded, and the paper was stiff with age. Brian flipped the pages over, pretending to look at the other photographs for something to do.

'Do you want a different picture of Marilyn, Dennis?' said Pat.

'Yes, for a change,' said Jean. 'Do you want to choose another one? For a change?'

Dennis rolled his eyes and Brian hung the calendar back on its nail. Pat said she would make some tea, and Jean followed her out of the room.

'Those two never come up for air,' said Dennis.

'They mean well.'

'Asking about my wishes. Wishes, for fuck's sake. On and on. And the nurses go on about it. Do I want to be buried? Or cremated? Shit like that. What do I care? Been on about wills and all sorts. All anyone really cares about these days is money.'

Getting the words out was an effort, and his head fell back onto the pillows.

Brian didn't know what to say. He wanted his sisters to come back with a teapot and cups and saucers and biscuits on a tray. He wanted to hear them chattering again. He looked out of the window. The sun was shining on the house across the way.

'It's a nice day,' he said.

But Dennis didn't say anything. He looked up at the ceiling, maybe at the light fitting. Or maybe at nothing at all. There was that look in his eyes, as if he was still stuck up that tree. As if all he could see was the end of the road.

*

Dennis died in hospital a week later. Brian went over to the house to see what needed to be done. Pat's fella, Johnny, was wearing work gloves and pulling stuff out of the old shed.

'Got to clear it out and take it down. Regulations. Because it's not part of the original property. Some stupid shit like that.'

'It's been falling down for years,' said Brian. 'We used to call it The Hut. It was Dad's hidey-hole before he died. What's in there now?' He poked his head through the door. Old paint cans and some rotting carpet. It stank of damp. 'We need a skip. Get a skip and just get rid of it all.'

'Stan said he wants any metal for scrap. Always looking to collect scrap is your Stan. Sells it somewhere.'

Brian didn't want to see his brother Stan. There was bad blood between them. Always had been. Stan was always wanting to put him down, and used to kick him in bed when he came home drunk. When Brian joined the army, he thought he'd come back one day and show them, show Stan, what he'd made of himself. So he'd turned up in a left-hand drive Opel Manta, with bronze paintwork and a black vinyl roof. He'd driven it all the way from Germany with Ute, who was pregnant and fearful about moving to a village in a part of England she'd never heard of: Weardale in County Durham.

And Stan had been determined to cause trouble, always bothering Ute. Calling her a Kraut Bitch behind her back. And then trying it on with her, getting her into corners when they were out drinking in the pubs at weekends. Never leaving off. Brian started thinking they were at it. Called Ute a slut and got himself into a right state. So he couldn't blame her for packing up and leaving.

And taking little Helmut with her. But really, Brian blamed Stan. Thought he'd planned it like that. Knew it.

He'd done well in the army, but always being posted from one place to another unsettled him. And he'd started thinking that where he was from was where he belonged. He came back to a good job at the cement works up the dale. Management. But after a few years a French company bought it up, and he was made redundant when they closed it down. Now he was stuck here, caught up in it, the family and all it meant. Ute was living in Berlin now. In a city, she'd written, people aren't so stupid.

'Stan's coming here then, is he?' said Brian.

'Didn't I say? He's coming to take the junk away in his trailer. He wants any metal for scrap. So, we won't need a skip,' said Johnny, going back inside the shed. 'Oh dear.' He laughed and came out with a pile of magazines and made a show of them to Brian. 'Girly mags.' They both pretended not to be interested in the pictures of pouting young women in their underwear. 'So the dirty old bugger had a porn collection. Heh, heh. Do you think he came out here to…you know?'

Brian smelled the damp and rot coming from inside the shed. 'Probably best not to think about that. It would put you off, wouldn't it? Standing in there with your jolly roger hanging out.'

'I've had a piss in worse places.'

'What else is in there?'

'There's this,' said Johnny, and dragged out a small anvil. 'Pretty good piece of kit. Useful.'

'Stan'll want that for scrap. He'd rather have the money than the use of it.'

Johnny gave him a look. 'Stan doesn't have to know about it. Does he, Brian? What the eye doesn't see…I could use this in my workshop. Mind, it's a weight.'

Brian helped Johnny carry the anvil and lift it into the boot of Johnny's Mondeo.

'Not a word to Stan, eh?'

'We don't have many words these days. Maybe a grunt now and again, or a special nod at Christmas. If we're in a festive mood. Otherwise...'

'You lot. I never know who's talking to who sometimes. Pat and Jean weren't talking till this business with Dennis. You know, with him getting the cancer...Bad business. Pat's in bits.'

Brian went into the house. Pat was in the kitchen, sitting at the table next to the television, at the far end of the room. She was sorting through some papers.

'Bank statements, bills,' she said. 'But he wouldn't make a will. Didn't see the point. Wouldn't even talk about it. Even though he knew. Well, he knew what was coming.'

'Didn't want to think about it, I suppose.' Brian remembered the look in Dennis's eyes. 'Couldn't face the thought.'

'I don't know how they missed the bloody cancer. That came out of the blue. I mean he had that problem with his chest. That was bad enough. Coughing his guts out. Always going to see the consultant. I know. I drove him there. Now I'm thinking, why didn't they test for it? Medical negligence. That's what it is. And now there's this to deal with.' She pushed the papers around. 'It's a mess. And we've got to clear the house. And there's the funeral to organise. And it's all got to be paid for.'

'He had money though, didn't he? In the bank?'

Pat picked up one of the sheets of paper and looked at it. 'Oh, there's money in his account, alright. But how do we get hold of it?'

'A man can pay for his own funeral. Can't he?'

'What? Even if he's dead?'

'It should be allowed. It's his money and it's his body. Call the bank. Ask them.'

Brian decided to look around the house to see what had to be cleared out. To see, he knew, if there was anything he wanted. He looked in the kitchen cupboards, at the plates and bowls that his mother had used, that he'd eaten off so many times. In the pantry was a box of cornflakes, a box of Kellogg's Cornflakes. He recognised the bright colours, the red and green cartoon of a cock crowing. He reached for it. Something felt wrong. He put it back on the shelf and made a noise, as if he'd been bitten.

'What's wrong?' said Pat.

'Cornflakes,' he said. 'Kellogg's Cornflakes.'

'So?'

'Haven't had them since I was a kid. Did you like them back then? With cold milk. Proper full fat. Not this semi-skimmed stuff.'

'Stan will be here soon,' she said. 'At least he'll know what to do.'

'About what?'

'About clearing out the house.'

'I told you. Get a skip and throw it all out,' said Brian, looking at the china in the display cabinet. 'This stuff? Nobody wants this sort of stuff now. Even Mam never used it. I know I don't want it. Do you want it? Really?'

'It needs to be sorted,' she said. 'If there's anything you want, just take it.'

Brian went into the sitting room and looked at the piles of newspapers and magazines on the floor. He called out to Pat.

'Why did he have all these newspapers, for fuck's sake?'

'He never got around to throwing them out,' she said. 'He didn't like to throw things out.'

'You'll need a skip,' said Brian, and went upstairs.

His parents' old bedroom looked as it always had, his mother's dressing table set with her brush and a few familiar family photographs. The double bed was made up, the cover smoothed down as if they were still sleeping there. As if they were still alive.

In his brother's bedroom the sheets had been pulled off the bed, and there was a stain on the mattress. Dennis's dark suit was hanging behind the door in a clear plastic bag from the dry cleaners, and there were boxes of pills and tubs of cream on the bedside table.

In the drawer, he found a crumpled mess of letters. He saw the NHS logo, and looked through them. They were from a consultant, saying there was a good chance Dennis had bowel cancer and he needed to have a colonoscopy. In one, the consultant said he was disappointed that Dennis had felt he was bothering him when he'd phoned. 'I urge you to reconsider…' he'd written.

He stuffed the letters back in the drawer, leaving them for Pat to find. It was too difficult to tell her that Dennis had kept the whole thing to himself, and refused help because he had been too frightened. Of a colonoscopy. Of cancer. Of knowing how he was going to die. It was the way his brother was. He thought that if he ignored things, didn't speak about them, they would disappear.

Brian wanted a piss, and went into the bathroom, but a contraption had been fitted around the toilet, and he didn't want to be bothered with it. Couldn't face it, really, like the stain on the mattress.

He went into the small back bedroom to look at the framed photograph of the red canoe hanging over the narrow bed. He'd wanted to see it again, the picture of the blue lake under a blue sky, with the snow-capped mountains in the distance. The colours had faded, but a boy was still sitting in that red canoe, ready for adventure, with his paddle raised to strike the water.

He took the picture with him when he went downstairs. Jean was in the living room kneeling in front of the sideboard with the door open, pulling things out.

'There's an old picture of you when you were in the army,' she said, holding it up. 'Very handsome.'

He glanced at the black and white photograph, and saw himself in his army uniform all those years ago, the toecaps of his boots shiny with spit and polish. Jean tried to hand it to him, but he shook his head. He didn't want it. But he stooped to root about in the drawers. He found an old wristwatch, the leather strap stiff with age. He tried the winder, but the works were all gummed up.

Dennis had kept all the things they'd forgotten, all the things that reminded them of the way they were. The more they looked in the cupboards and drawers, the more of it they'd find. But what good was any of it? All of it was useless, like the broken watch that had been his father's.

Brian didn't want to think about what there was to remember. The past had faded or turned to dust and was out of reach. He was unable to find his way back to it, like a drowning man can't reach the river bank as the current sweeps him away.

Pat was still at the kitchen table, still looking at the papers.

'Have you called the bank?' he said.

'No I haven't called the bank. Why would I want to call the bank?'

'To sort out the money for the funeral. From Dennis's account. I thought…'

'Stan'll be here soon. He'll know what to do.'

'I told Johnny,' he said. 'We need to get a skip. Order a skip for fuck's sake. Most of the stuff here is just junk. Just throw it out. It'll be easier.'

'Oh, you're full of it today, aren't you? Where were you when Dennis needed helping to the toilet? Or needed to be cleaned up because he'd made a mess of the bed? Where the fuck were you when there was actual shit to deal with?'

'I'm taking this picture,' he said, holding it up for her to see.

'You're not off, are you? Stan will be here soon.'

'Where is he, then? Where is Stan?' he said, tucking the picture under his arm.

'He'll be along. You'll see.'

Jean came through from the sitting room, waving a packet of cigarettes.

'Just found these fags,' she said.

'Won't they be stale?'

'Still sealed up in the packet. I'm going to try one out.'

She went outside and Brian opened the pantry door. He looked at the box of cornflakes.

'You're not still thinking about those fucking cornflakes, are you?' said Pat.

Stan came in before he could say anything, walking with his chest out and his head back. He wore a lumberjack shirt and pair of work pants held up with bright red braces.

'What's up, Corporal?'

Stan always called him 'Corporal' to annoy him. Brian had actually been a Warrant Officer when he left the army, but Stan didn't know what a fucking W.O. was. Because Stan didn't know fuck all.

'He's got a thing about cornflakes, Stanley,' said Pat. 'Tell him, Brian. Tell Stanley about the cornflakes.'

Brian didn't like the look that passed between them, like they were both enjoying a chance to take the piss. And whatever he said would make Pat think she'd made a fool of him. Stan was over by the table now, looking down at the papers Pat had in front of her. He put his hands in his pockets and looked at Brian.

'So, what's the thing about cornflakes, Corporal?'

'Kellogg's Cornflakes. We used to have them when we were kids. Don't you remember?'

'Why don't you just take them, Brian?' said Pat. 'I mean, if it'll make you happy. A box of bloody cornflakes, for fuck's sake.'

'You always were a tight bastard, Corporal…' Stan picked up a few of Dennis's bank statements and leafed through them. 'This isn't right, Pat. He had more than this. All that cash from when he went beating.'

Dennis used to go beating for the Arabs who owned the shooting rights on the moors. They came every August to shoot grouse. And they paid in cash, with big bonuses to all the men. Everyone in the family knew. It was the only thing Dennis ever boasted about.

'Maybe there's another account,' said Pat.

Another look passed between her and Stan.

'We need to clear the house, Stanley. And pay for the funeral.'

'Get a skip. And call the bank. They'll sort it.'

'I said that,' said Brian. 'That they can't stop a man paying for his own funeral. Even if he's dead.'

'Even if he's dead, Corporal. Did you really say that? What a clever boy. Mam always said you were a clever boy. Didn't she?'

'I'll take the cornflakes, then. And the picture. I don't want anything else.'

Stan asked him to hold up the picture.

'You always had a thing about that photo. Always on about going to Canada. But you never went, did you?'

Jean was standing by the shed when he left, smoking and talking to Johnny.

'You taking the cornflakes?' she said.

'You taking the cigarettes?'

'Why not?'

'You see Stanley?' said Johnny. 'You didn't say anything, did you?'

'What about?' said Jean.

'Nothing,' said Brian. 'You know me and Stan.'

He walked down the garden and didn't mind if they thought he was slinking off. He was glad to be out of there, not just away from Stan and Pat, but away from the house and the smell of it. Let the rest of them pick over what was left.

*

Brian sat at his kitchen table and looked at the picture of the red canoe. The glass was coated in dust. He wiped it with a dampened dishcloth, but the frame came apart in his hands, and he nicked his finger on the edge of the glass. Sucking at the cut, he saw what the picture had become. The memory of a dream.

He poured himself a large glass of Irish whiskey and sat facing the window. He sat there for a long time, until the light faded. And he was still sitting in the dark when the lights came on in Dennis's house. Someone was moving around in the rooms, upstairs and downstairs. Stan, he thought, looking for Dennis's money.

Brian drained his whiskey off, drew the curtains and switched on the light. He filled a bowl with Dennis's cornflakes, and poured cold milk over them. They tasted stale, and he spat them back into the bowl. But it wasn't the cornflakes. It was the packet he really wanted. He grabbed hold of it, and after taking out the inner bag, he tipped the box up, letting what had been hidden inside fall onto the table. Five, six, no seven, rolls of banknotes, each held together with an elastic band.

He separated the ten, twenty and fifty-pound notes into neat piles. And as he counted out the money, he thought about Stan tearing the house apart and finding nothing. He imagined his brother going out into the garden in the middle of the night, with a torch and a spade, and digging one pointless hole after another.

Brian had over ten thousand pounds on his kitchen table, and Stan was dreaming of buried treasure. It was a good joke.

The Bermuda Triangle

Sarah poured herself a glass of wine. She drank it standing at the breakfast bar, and when the glass was half empty she topped it up. After all, she deserved a drink. Tonight another bulb had blown in the overhead lighting track. In the half-light, she noticed the glow of the microwave oven, and saw the pasta meal for one turning inside it. Tom would have called it a 'ping dinner'. She laughed at the thought, but something caught on the memory.

She'd known, even before the accident. It was in the way he turned away from her sometimes, or kissed her too quickly. Or in the way he avoided sex by being too drunk or too tired. And there was a change in the petty cruelties of their relationship. He no longer responded to her goading him about his lack of ambition, or what she called his 'silver spoon', and he stopped calling her 'fat' or 'stupid' or 'working class'. It had all been replaced with indifference.

When the police had given her Tom's things from the wreckage of the car she'd put them back where he kept them; in the wardrobe, or in the desk in the little room he used as a study.

Except for his phone. She put that in the junk drawer, the one in the kitchen he used to call The Bermuda Triangle, because that's where all the lost things ended up. But it didn't stay lost. She'd fished it out and charged the battery.

She'd told herself she only wanted to see the last photographs he'd taken of her. But she knew what she was really after when she switched it on and tapped in his PIN. And there it was, in an unopened text message, received on the day of the accident. 'Tom,' it read, 'where were you today? The scan is wonderful. Please call. I love you, Kaja xxx.' The fact of it had curled up inside her, and was always there, behind every thought. It ruined every memory.

As she drank the wine too quickly, her eyes flicked to her own phone lying on the worktop as it began to vibrate. She snatched it up even before it started to ring. It was Mary, Tom's mother.

'How are you?'

'Fine,' said Sarah.

'It's difficult, isn't it?'

'I was just thinking about Tom. Remembering him.'

'You must have so many good memories,' said Mary.

'The flat feels so empty.'

'Come and stay.'

'What?'

'Come up tomorrow. For the weekend. Colin would love to see you. Have you got anything on?'

'I don't know.'

'Please. Let me help. Please say you'll come.'

There was a promise in Mary's voice, in her sweet beguiling tone, and Sarah said yes, of course she'd love to come.

The alarm on the microwave pinged. Sarah screwed the cap back on the bottle of wine and pushed it away from her. She wanted to have a clear head in the morning and spend Friday looking forward to the weekend, just like everyone else.

The next day, as autumn sunshine cut across the foyer of the building where she worked, she stood, takeaway coffee in hand, waiting for the lift.

'Hey, Sarah.' It was Laura. 'Fancy going for a drink after work? Just the two of us.'

'I can't. Tom's mother wants me to go up for the weekend. She's still in a bad way.'

'She's got some nerve.'

Laura was an old friend, and when they'd had a few drinks after work Sarah used to moan about 'the mother-in-law'. But she didn't want to be reminded about how she used to talk about Mary. Not now. She looked up at the display to see what floor the lift was on.

'I've promised her,' she said. 'I can't wait for this bloody lift.' She turned to Laura as she pushed open the door to the stairwell. 'We'll get together soon. I promise.'

*

Sarah guided the Volkswagen along the drive. Mature shrubs kept the house from view until she rounded the final bend and it appeared to her all at once; a former vicarage, stone built and double fronted. Low stone steps led up to a wide door, painted pale green with a brass knocker in the shape of a lion's head.

A Range Rover was parked in front of the house and she pulled up behind it. A black Labrador rushed out, wagging its tail. It followed her as she went to the boot to get her bag. Mary appeared and Colin, Tom's father, came behind her. He held back as Mary embraced Sarah, and she sensed his embarrassment. She kissed him quickly on the cheek, feeling his evening stubble against her lips and catching the faint smell of aftershave as he took the bag from her hand.

'Welcome, my darling,' said Mary, putting an arm around her. 'Let's get you inside.'

Mary's hair was coloured, Sarah knew, to conceal the grey. And her figure was gym toned; she wore a fitted black woollen dress, the colour softened by a long necklace of polished amber, and tan suede boots. As Sarah passed the mirror in the hallway she glimpsed her own reflection; her anorak and her crumpled t-shirt, her tangled hair and her tired eyes.

'I'm so glad to be here,' she said.

'You must think of this as your home. That's what Tom would have wanted, isn't it?'

After the accident they'd invited her up to plan the funeral. She'd taken compassionate leave and stayed with them, spending time with Mary looking through photographs and listening to some of Tom's favourite music. They got a little drunk sometimes and stopped being embarrassed about crying, as they sat on one of the huge sofas in the lounge, Sarah with her feet tucked under a cushion, leaning against Mary as she turned the pages of the photograph album.

She took her bag up to the guest room and had a shower, brushed her hair, put on some make up and changed into a dress. When she came back down Mary was in the kitchen, standing at the granite worktop wearing a blue and white striped apron.

'Can I help?' said Sarah.

'No, it's alright. You relax.'

'I'd like to.'

'Pour me some wine, then.'

'I could do the carrots.' Sarah saw them in a large bowl, peeled and glistening under the spotlights.

'Can you cut them into juliennes?'

'I'm not sure what they are.'

'You do it like this.' Mary picked up a knife, took one of the carrots, cut it in half lengthways and turned it on to the flat side. Her knife moved quickly and the carrot became a pile of thin strips. 'They need to be about two inches long,' she said.

'Oh yes. I see,' said Sarah. 'Like matchsticks.'

'Yes, if you like. But they're called juliennes.'

'Do you want red wine?'

'No, there's some Picpoul in the fridge. I'll have that.'

After she'd poured them both a glass of wine, Sarah picked up the knife and began to cut one of the carrots in the way she had been shown. She knew she was being watched, and looked up. Mary smiled at her.

'This is nice,' she said. 'Us. In the kitchen together.'

After dinner, the two of them sat on one of the sofas in the sitting room, just as they had before Tom's funeral. They were looking at the album again. Mary turned the pages and told Sarah stories she'd heard before, but she didn't mind hearing them again. She wanted to share Mary's idea of Tom, wanted to hold it inside her so she could mourn him, not just as someone she had loved, but who had loved her.

Colin kept to his study, looking in on them now and again to make sure they had enough wine or to put another log on the fire. As he topped up their glasses, Mary broke off from telling one of her stories. 'We really mean it when we say we think of you as part of this family. Don't we, Colin?'

Colin said something in affirmation. It sounded like a grunt.

'If you and Tom had got married,' said Mary. 'And we all knew you would, didn't we?' She reached out and touched Sarah's hand. 'He was all we had, wasn't he?' And she burst into tears.

Sarah put her arm around Mary and looked up at Colin. He froze with the wine bottle in his hand, as if he thought he'd been invisible, and suddenly realised she could see him. He gave her a quick, nervous smile.

'You're more or less our daughter-in-law,' said Mary. 'I mean he loved you so much. You were part of his life. You must know you're part of ours now.'

'It's time for bed,' said Colin.

Mary delivered herself to him. He put his arm around her and led her upstairs. Sarah went into the kitchen, realising how much she wanted to feel at home in this house, as if she really was a part of it. Colin came back downstairs and found her loading the dishwasher.

'You don't need to do that,' he said.

'I feel so useless.' She noticed he was looking at her as if there was something he wanted to say.

'You help keep Tom alive for Mary.'

'Perhaps she does that for me, too.'

'Yes,' he said. 'I suppose that's it.' If there was something else he wanted to say, he'd decided against it, and said goodnight.

After breakfast Sarah and Mary went for a walk. Leaving the house through the French doors, they went across the lawn on a path of flagstones set into the grass like stepping stones. The dog ran ahead of them, towards the end of the garden where, beyond a white fence, was a thick wood. Sarah thought the fence seemed too pretty, too dainty to hold the trees at bay.

Tom had told her he used to call it the 'Wild Wood' when he was a boy and Mary told her the same story as she opened the gate onto a path through the trees. On either side was dense undergrowth; a tangle of brambles and dying ferns.

'I'm sorry about last night,' said Mary, as the dog roamed ahead of them. 'I was a little tired and emotional, wasn't I? It's getting to be a bit of a habit.'

'I get a little tired and emotional myself these days.'

'It's not easy. I know it isn't,' said Mary. 'But Tom thought you were special. And so do I.'

She put her arm through Sarah's and they walked together.

'Do you remember the other funny names he had for things?' said Mary.

'Oh yes, when I first met him…'

'When he was a boy he was always losing things. Said they were in The Bermuda Triangle. And gone forever.'

'Oh yes,' said Sarah, remembering the phone, at the bottom of her bag in the guest room. She looked up at the leafless branches of the trees against the white sky. Even here, under Mary's protection, the wrong Tom haunted her.

After lunch the two of them went to look around an antique shop. At first Sarah followed Mary, looking at what she looked at, half listening to her commentary. But when Mary went to talk with the dealer, she was left to herself.

She peered in through the windows of a large doll's house and pulled on the front wall, covered in paper brickwork. It swung open on hinges like a door. Now she saw all the rooms at once, with tables and chairs and beds, and even a tiny jug and bowl on a miniature washstand. She wished she could fit inside the house, and be one of those stiff wooden figures: mother, father, child or servant; every one of them in their place.

Later, they were sitting at the kitchen table drinking tea, and Mary said she had something Sarah would love to see. She fetched a large envelope, almost bulging beyond what it could hold, and tipped its contents out onto the table.

'These are all the cards people sent when he was in hospital,' she said. 'He touched so many people's lives, you know. Not just ours.'

Sarah held her breath as she looked at the cards, a pile of disorder in the middle of the clean, glossy kitchen. She knew what lay there, in amongst the pretty pictures of flowers, the sweet sentiments and the heartfelt scrawls.

Mary picked up cards at random, reading out the message and the name on each one. Sarah looked through them because she knew Mary wanted her to join in. She opened them and read them quickly and tossed them back on the table. Then she found it, with its image of a cat jumping across a blue sky. The handwriting was small, with carefully formed letters, 'I pray for you every day. With all my love, Kaja xxx.'

Realising Mary's attention was elsewhere, Sarah slipped Kaja's card down onto her lap, and then pushed it up under her sweater.

'I feel tired,' she said. 'Do you mind if I go and lie down?'

'Oh, darling. I'm sorry. It's so hard sometimes, isn't it?'

She nodded and went upstairs. In the bedroom she took the card out from under her sweater, and without looking at it, trying not to look at it, she tore it in two and then in two again, and then again. She tried flushing the pieces down the toilet in the en-suite bathroom, but the fragments of 'all my love Kaja, kiss, kiss, kiss' swirled around the pan, refusing to go away.

The room made her feel as if she was a guest in an upmarket country house hotel. Everything matched and everything was in its place. She took Tom's phone out of her bag and switched it on. She looked at the message again, hoping, as she did every time she read it, that she had made some stupid mistake. But now she realised she had lost him in every way, and what made her special to Mary, that Tom had loved her best, wasn't true.

She went downstairs with the phone in her hand. Looking for Mary, determined to tell her, she wandered from room to room and out into the garden. She walked down the lawn to the fence, and went through the gate and into the wood, striking off the path without knowing where she was going. Brambles tore at her clothes, ripped her tights and scratched her legs. Something cut into her face.

Colin was walking back to the house with the dog when he saw her. Seeing the state she was in, he quickened his step. She saw Tom in him, in the set of his jaw and the way he walked, and she stumbled through the undergrowth towards him in a blundering fury. Sensing her anger, he caught her by the wrists as she tried to flail at him.

'He was seeing someone else,' she said.

'I know.'

Colin put his arm around her and guided her back along the path and into the house. Mary was wandering around the living room with a glass of white wine in her hand. On seeing Sarah, dishevelled and bleeding, she cried out.

'What's happened?'

'Your little Tommy wasn't such a lovely boy,' said Sarah. 'He was seeing another woman. She's expecting his baby.'

Sarah held Tom's mobile out in front of her with Kaja's message on the screen. Mary took it from her, staggering a little because she was drunk, and sat down. She worked the keypad of the phone and put it to her ear.

'Kaja? Is that Kaja?'

'Oh, so that's how you say it. It's such a pretty name.' She listened for a moment, sipping her wine, and twirling the glass by its stem. 'I'm Tom's mother,' she said, 'We've just found his phone and read your message. You poor darling.'

Sarah stood, clenching and unclenching her fists, unsteady on her feet. Exhausted. Her anger was not enough; she struggled to keep her eyes open. They began to flutter, to close against her will. Her eyeballs rolled upwards under the lids, as if she was trying to look inside her own head. And from far, far away she heard Mary's voice. Not the words, only its sweet, beguiling tone as she fell into darkness.

Cabaret

The four of them managed to get a table with a view of La Rocca. They were trying to catch the waiter's eye, when Carlo Bellazzo walked out onto the terrace. Nigel stared at him.

'What kind of hairstyle is that?' he said.

'It's called a man bun,' said Magda. 'It's very fashionable, apparently.'

'Well, it's ridiculous,' said Nigel. 'Absolutely ridiculous.'

Steve laughed. 'You really do hate him, don't you?'

'Can't you just change rooms?' said Anna. 'It's spoiling your holiday.'

'That's not the point,' said Magda.

Nigel noticed how the waiter rushed over to take Carlo's order. Steve was right, he hated Carlo Bellazzo and his electronic keyboard. Accompanied by a guitarist and a drum machine, he played pop covers in the hotel lounge from nine o'clock every night. The sound echoed around the courtyard. Trying to persuade Magda to close the windows and forget about it didn't help. Because that wasn't the point, was it? They'd paid for a room with a balcony.

On the second night, as Carlo sang 'Delilah' and the crowd joined in the chorus, Magda paced their room, moaning her nerves were on fire. Nigel tried to persuade her to take a stroll along the promenade into Cefalu, and have an ice cream or a drink at one of the bars. But she couldn't help herself, and complained that her dream of sitting on the balcony in the evening air had been destroyed by what she called 'this ridiculous cabaret'.

They complained to the tour company rep, a Frenchwoman, who sat in the hotel dining room every morning with a card machine and a pile of brochures, waiting to take bookings for optional excursions. Magda began speaking to her in French (she prided herself on her fluency) and the woman muttered something under her breath. Nigel thought it sounded like 'merde'. In the end, probably because there was a queue building up behind them, she agreed to arrange a meeting with the hotel manager.

Later, the rep collected them from their sun loungers by the pool, and led them down the corridor towards reception. She wore a fitted floral dress and carried a large handbag like the Italian women Nigel had seen in Palermo. The faster she walked, and the more insistent the rhythm of her high heels, the more his all-terrain sandals squeaked on the marble floor as they hurried after her. He remembered the day he had followed the boss's PA down another corridor. The day he was told that early retirement was an opportunity he shouldn't refuse.

The manager was waiting for them in reception and invited them into his office. Hanging above his desk was a large framed photograph of Carlo stripped to the waist, his muscular torso glistening with oil. It was signed, with kisses. Nigel hadn't really heard the manager's name properly, it had just been a burst of

Italian syllables, but now he saw it on the brass plate on the desk in front of him: Luca Bellazzo. There was a familial resemblance about the jaw line, and although Carlo dressed in flowing shirts and the manager wore an immaculate pale blue suit, both men were possessed of a natural, arrogant elegance.

Nigel began to feel hot, even though he was wearing shorts. His pale legs started sticking to the leather chair as he began to explain their predicament. Magda took over, strident in the way she always was, speaking in French because she had no Italian. The manager glanced at her and then looked at Nigel. It was a particular kind of look, and he knew what it meant. 'Can't you control your wife?' That's what it meant.

'Does the music happen after midnight?' said the manager.

'Sometimes it doesn't stop until after one o'clock,' said Nigel.

'Carlo is very popular with the other guests. They always want more.'

'It's not fair,' said Magda.

'You want another room?'

'With a balcony? We paid for a room with a balcony.'

The manager glanced at his computer and shook his head.

'Change rooms,' said the rep.

'Can't you do something?' said Magda as they walked back to the pool.

'What do you mean?'

'I don't know, Nigel. Something. Just do something.'

That evening, as they were having after dinner drinks on the terrace, Nigel leaned over the table towards Steve.

'Do you think you could come with me to see the manager? You know, it might help if we went a bit mob-handed.'

'I don't want to get involved,' said Steve. 'Complaining about something that's not really bothering me. I don't want to spoil my holiday by getting all hot under the collar. Neither should you. I doubt the hotel will do anything about it. Carlo's good for bar sales, after all.'

'Perhaps you should just change rooms,' said Anna. 'It might be for the best.'

'That's not the point,' said Magda.

Nigel stood up. Supposedly on his way to the toilet, he took a detour through the lounge where Carlo's equipment had been set up for the night. He stopped and looked at it with his hands in his pockets, as if he was just curious. Of course, he didn't really know what he was looking at. After checking there was no one around to see him, he went up to the nearest amplifier, pulled out three cables at random, and dropped them onto the floor. Then he stamped on the jack plugs until the soles of his heavy-duty sandals shattered the plastic, and the wiring came away.

At nine o'clock, there was no music. Nigel didn't say anything, and as they seemed unable to attract the attention of the waiter yet again, he volunteered to go inside and buy another round. Because he hadn't ordered through the waiter, he had to enter into a curious ritual with the cashier; queueing at the cash desk, giving her his order, paying for it and taking the receipt over to the bar. Anna came, she said, to help him carry the drinks, and they waited for the barman to notice them.

'It's a very quaint system, isn't it?'

'It's very Italian,' he said, trying to get the barman's attention. 'It can't be rushed.'

'Apparently not,' said Anna. 'Are you having such an awful time?'

'It's not all bad,' he said, smiling at her. He liked the way she tucked her hair behind her ear when she talked.

'It's funny how you get together with people on holiday, isn't it?' she said. 'We'll probably exchange addresses and say "let's keep in touch."'

'Yes,' said Nigel.

'But most people never bother, do they?'

The barman noticed them at last, and as he fixed their drinks Nigel heard music coming from the other room. Carlo was singing 'Out of Time'. He must have had spare cables; he was nothing if not professional.

The next evening, they got back from the excursion to Mount Etna and went out onto the terrace for drinks. Magda was in a mood because Nigel had refused to pay fifty euros for a ride up to the summit in a Land Rover. Of course, Steve and Anna had gone, and Steve was full of it. He told Magda she would have loved it.

'I know,' she said.

Nigel said he was off to the loo, and passed through the lounge where, once again, the sound equipment was set up. He had thought about it all day, how water and electricity didn't mix. It was meant to be dangerous. He made sure he was alone, took a small plastic bottle of mineral water from the pocket of his cargo shorts, and emptied it over one of the amplifiers. He dropped the bottle onto the floor. Whatever happened when the power was switched on, he imagined sparks or even a small explosion, would look like an accident.

He hung around the bar, pretending to look at the cakes in the display fridge, until he saw Carlo and his guitarist walk through, into the lounge. He stood in the doorway to watch. The singer was about to switch on the amplifier, but he hesitated, felt along the top of it and rubbed his fingers together. He saw the water bottle, picked it up and shouted out to the other man. They stood and talked for a moment. Carlo shrugged his shoulders, and the man went off. He came back with a trolley and they loaded the amplifier onto it. Nigel knew, just knew, they had another one, in a storeroom in the hotel, or in a van parked outside the building. He went to join the others on the terrace. A few minutes later he heard the beat of the drum machine and the opening bars of 'Satisfaction'.

The next day they had an early start to take a tour of Agrigento. As soon as she got on the coach Magda complained of a headache. Steve was, as ever, wearing his headphones around his neck, and was keen to show them to her. They were noise cancelling. Get a pair of these, he told her, and you won't have a problem. She asked if they were expensive.

'If you knew me better, you'd know that I only buy the best,' Steve said.

'That's my husband,' said Anna. 'Only the best is good enough.'

'Well, what's the point otherwise?'

'Oh, I know that's true,' said Magda. 'Cheap's just another word for waste of money, isn't it? We've just had a new kitchen. And I wasn't prepared to skimp. Was I, Nigel?'

Magda and Steve chatted over the back of the seat about the virtues of granite worktops over cheaper alternatives. Nigel looked out of the window. Poor Magda, he thought. She hadn't come to terms with his early retirement, that awful euphemism for redundancy; the loss of funds and social status had hit her hard. The kitchen had been his conciliatory gift to her. The last thing she had to show off about.

The coach passed an abandoned building project, and he wondered how much of his lump sum would be left in six months. This holiday was blatantly not the best. Price had been his main, actually it had been his only consideration, and now he was unlikely to hear the last of it. Carlo Bellazzo was just the latest drop of rain on his parade.

It was hot in Agrigento. Nigel and Anna walked together, listening intently to the guide, as she led them past the ruins of Greek temples. Steve and Magda lagged behind, deep in conversation. Their critique of the modern kitchen now touched upon the subject of induction hobs, and it seemed as if they had no time for the ancient world.

That evening, the two couples, who had never met until they were forced to share a table in the hotel dining room every night, once again sat on the terrace for after dinner drinks. Carlo was sipping a glass of prosecco a few tables away. Once again, Nigel gave up trying to attract the attention of the waiter. He said he was going to the toilet and would order more drinks on his way back. He took a detour through the lounge. Sitting next to the sound equipment was a young man in t-shirt and jeans looking at his mobile phone. He looked up at Nigel, smiled and went back to his texting. Carlo had posted a guard.

Nigel went to order the drinks. He said good evening to the woman behind the cash desk in Italian, but she conducted the entire transaction in silence, pointing to the amount he owed on the till display. Anna joined him at the bar.

'We can't hear the music in our room,' she said.

'It's only the rooms that overlook the courtyard,' said Nigel. 'And then it's only us who are bothered by it. I don't blame Steve. Really, I don't.'

When they took the drinks to the table, Nigel noticed Steve give him a strange look, but he had other things on his mind. It was dark outside now, nearly time for the show to begin, and then Magda would start berating him for not being able to fix it, for being useless. For not doing anything.

THIRTEEN

When Carlo got up from his table and walked off the terrace through the gate that led into the garden, Nigel stood up. 'Call of nature,' he announced. He went through the bar, out of the door at the far end of the room, and came into the garden near the pool.

Carlo was standing on the lawn smoking a cigarette, silhouetted by the glow from the pool's underwater lights. Nigel hid behind a bush and watched him, trying to decide what to do. He looked around his feet for something he could use as a weapon, a branch or a rock. There was a child's spade made of yellow plastic, and he picked it up, knocking it against his other hand to check how hard it was. He steeled himself, and was getting ready to rush out, when he realised someone had come up beside him. It was Anna.

'What are you doing, Nigel?'

'I don't know,' he said. 'Something?'

'Why don't we go into the town after this?'

'Magda won't go. She's stubborn.'

'I meant you and me,' she said. 'Can't we just slip off?'

They stood and watched Carlo. He tugged at his topknot and shook his hair loose. It fell to his shoulders and he combed it through with his fingers. Nigel realised how graceful the singer was, an exotic creature in black silk pyjamas. The thought made him feel shabby and ridiculous. Anna tugged at his arm and he dropped the spade.

They began to walk away. Nigel wasn't sure where they were going. He was trying to orientate himself when he was knocked forward. Despite the shock he managed to regain his balance and turn. Steve was coming at him with the plastic spade in his hand.

'Steve,' shouted Anna. 'Stop it.'

'You bastard,' said Steve, hitting out with the spade.

Nigel felt sharp stabbing pains on his forehead, as if he was being pecked by a bird. He raised his arms to protect his face and fell over backwards. Looking up, he saw Carlo rush across the grass, catch Steve by the arm and twist him down onto the ground in a single movement.

'A jealous husband?' Carlo said, grinning and holding out his hand to help Nigel to his feet. 'It happens to me, all the time.'

Later, on the terrace, Steve claimed he didn't know what had come over him. He blamed the heat in Agrigento that afternoon. Magda said she didn't know what the three of them were doing out in the garden in the first place. It was Anna who got a first aid kit from behind the bar, cleaned up Nigel's forehead with an antiseptic wipe and covered his wounds with a large plaster. She took the opportunity to tuck a piece of paper into his shirt pocket. He touched his fingers to his chest, feeling the note through the fabric.

They all heard the music, an urgent compelling beat. Nigel smiled. The others looked at him, as if they didn't know what to do. As if they thought he knew.

'It's time,' he said, getting to his feet. 'Time to go and watch Carlo strut his stuff.'

Flora and Fauna

The woman – early sixties, dyed blonde hair and rimless glasses – stood just inside the doorway of the coffee shop and looked around. She was getting in everyone's way; people leaving or coming in off the street kept bumping into her.

Robert recognised her from the photograph on the website, although she wasn't quite as big as he'd imagined. Perhaps it was like seeing someone famous on the street; they never looked the same as they did on television. He pushed himself up from his seat and raised his arm.

'Marilyn?'

'Robert?' She came over, offered her cheek for him to kiss, and dropped down onto the chair opposite his. 'I can't face that queue. Get me a skinny latte, would you?'

'Do you want a piece of cake, or something like that? A pastry?'

'I'm on a diet,' she said. 'Why else would I ask for a skinny latte?'

'I'm sorry. But you don't look as if you need to lose weight.'

'Really? Well, it is a date after all. Get me something with chocolate. I might as well be hung for a sheep as a lamb.'

He came back with the coffee and a wedge of gateau, and she said, 'You look older than your photograph.'

'It was the only one I had,' he said, pushing the plate towards her.

'You're not divorced, are you? There's always something wrong with the divorced ones. Bound to be.'

'I'm a widower,' he said.

'Ah, the widower,' she said. 'I'm divorced and I'm straight up about it. But men always lie. I've kissed enough frogs to know that. And I'm fed up with it.' She sighed and cut into the cake with the edge of her fork. 'Before we start, we need to agree rules.'

'Rules?'

'I have three rules,' she said. 'One. Don't ever call me. If I want to get in touch, I'll call you. You can't have my number. If you're not okay with that, let's call it off now. Okay?'

'Okay.'

'Rule number two. We only meet on neutral territory. Until we're sure. If we are ever going to be sure,' she said, lifting the fork towards her mouth.

'Number three,' he said. 'What's rule number three?'

She finished her mouthful of cake, and took a deep breath. 'Don't pester me for sex. Men always want sex. It's all you lot think about, isn't it?'

He didn't answer and looked around the coffee shop.

'These places are all the same, aren't they?'

*

She'd called him the week before. From a withheld number.

'You like art? Your profile says you do.'

'Oh, yes. Of course,' he'd said.

Signing up for the dating site had reminded him of filling in application forms when he was looking to go to university. They always wanted to know your interests. It was meant to show you were a well-rounded person. But what was there to put down? Cinema, music, walking, reading; the usual. He'd added cookery to his profile, which was true. And art, which wasn't.

'Then we should go and look at an exhibition.'

'Does that count as a date?'

'It's what couples do,' she'd said. 'It'll help us get to know each other.'

'I thought we'd go for dinner. Or a drink.'

'On the first date it's best if there's daylight. And no alcohol.'

*

They left the coffee shop and walked down to the art gallery, a converted industrial building on the regenerated riverside. Robert didn't know why Marilyn had thought this was a good idea; she seemed as uninterested as he was. Hardly speaking, they wandered from floor to floor and room to room, moving listlessly from one artwork to another.

Eventually, they sat on a wooden bench in front of a large video projection. On the screen a man in a business suit was pushing a round rock, about three metres in diameter, up a dry slope strewn with pebbles. His clothes were covered in dust as he fought for traction in the dirt, but no matter how hard and how long he pushed, he didn't seem to be getting any nearer to the top. Robert realised the footage was on a loop and got to his feet; he'd had enough. He thought Marilyn would take her cue from him, that she too was bored, but her eyes remained fixed on the struggling figure, and he sat back down.

'It's conceptual art,' he said, and she looked at him. 'It's the idea that counts. The rock's probably made of papier-mâché. Or polystyrene. He's only pretending.'

'He reminds me of my ex-husband,' said Marilyn. 'Neil made out he was a bloody martyr. But he wasn't. He was a chemical engineer. I thought he'd be a better catch than someone more poetic. I got all the fitted kitchens I wanted. So, I suppose I shouldn't moan. But it got to be so boring. And then he left me when the youngest went to university. For someone who shared his interests, he said. What interests? That's what I'd like to know.'

They got up together and stood in silence to read a large printed panel explaining the work. They turned to each other, and she wrinkled her nose.

'I like the Impressionists,' she said. 'This modern stuff's too clever for me.'

'It's all postmodernism now,' he said, 'Do you like Van Gogh?'

'He's alright,' she said, looking at her watch.

*

Robert pushed and pulled the vacuum cleaner over the hall carpet. He was enjoying the thought of all the dust and dirt being sucked up from amongst the pattern of tiny flowers, as if he was a gardener tending to his blooms.

His phone rang and broke his concentration. A withheld number. He thought it was more telesales and was ready to be irritated, but it was Marilyn. He wasn't just surprised. He was overjoyed.

'I didn't think it was that bad, was it?' she said. 'I mean, I've been thinking it wasn't bad for a first date. Definitely some chemistry there. Well, I thought so. Didn't you?'

'Yes,' he said. 'It was nice.'

'First dates are not really long enough, are they?'

'I suppose not.'

'Take it from me,' she said. 'Are you ready to take this to the next level?'

'What's that?'

'Dinner date.'

'Oh, yes.'

'I've got a good feeling about us, Robert. Have you?'

'Yes, I think I have, Marilyn.'

When she rang off, he stood in the living room and looked at the large black and white photograph of Alison over the fireplace. He loved the picture; the satin gown; her dyed blonde hair; her lips like a dark, tight bud, even though her eyes seemed glazed and unfocused.

'That was Marilyn on the phone,' he said. 'I think things have been a little difficult for her. And you know how that makes people, don't you?'

*

'Have you got any other dates lined up?' she said.

They were in a bar near the restaurant. She was knocking the ice and lemon around the bottom of her glass with a plastic twizzle stick.

'No,' he said. 'Just you.'

She looked up at him and smiled.

'Be a love and get me another, will you? We've still got time.'

'Aren't you drinking, then?' she said, when he came back from the bar, with her gin and a bottle of tonic, but nothing for himself.

'I haven't finished this one,' he said, and made a thing of knocking back some of his lager.

'My husband could go for weeks without a drink,' she said, 'He was a pious bastard when it suited him.'

'This beer's too gassy,' he said.

'Do you want a short, then. A whisky?' She grabbed her handbag and stood up. 'My treat.'

'Make it a g and t,' he said. 'I don't really like whisky.'

THIRTEEN

They were late getting to the restaurant, but a waitress showed them straight to a table, and when she brought the menus, Marilyn asked her to bring a bottle of Pinot Grigio. 'Straight away,' she said.

Robert didn't like the waiter. One too many buttons on his shirt were undone, and he fussed over Marilyn, asking her what 'the beautiful signora' would like. And he made crude gestures with an enormous pepper mill he brought to grind over her pasta. But she lapped it up.

Marilyn said she was optimistic about the future. And was thinking about joining a gym. Or a walking group. She asked if he'd heard anything about intermittent fasting. She talked as she ate and sauce dribbled onto her chin. Robert reached over to dab it off with his napkin.

'You're sweet,' she said, reaching across the table and squeezing his hand. 'You're a real gentleman.'

They went to a second bottle of wine and after dessert she ordered a Sambuca. When it came there was a coffee bean floating in it.

'Come on baby, light my fire,' said the waiter, flicking a disposable lighter to set the drink alight.

Marilyn giggled and Robert smiled, pretending his attention was, like hers, drawn to the bright blue flame. But he'd hated the way the waiter had flirted with her, and told her to blow it out.

'Already?' she said.

'Blow it out and make a wish. It's meant to be lucky.'

Marilyn blew the flame out.

'There,' she said, squeezing his hand. 'I made a wish.'

Marilyn was a little unsteady on her feet when they left the restaurant, and gripped Robert's arm as they walked towards the taxi rank. At the crossing, she pushed up against him.

'Let's go to a hotel,' she said. 'And see if my wish will come true.'

'We could go to my place,' he said. 'Or yours.'

'Neutral territory, Robert,' she said. 'That's one of the rules.'

They went to the hotel next to the station. As they walked up the steps to the entrance, Robert wondered if the receptionist would notice they had no luggage. He was ready with some story about missing the last train to somewhere. But the young woman, smart in a dark jacket and white shirt, just pushed the card machine towards him.

'Breakfast's from seven thirty until ten,' she said, handing him a key card. 'In the dining room.' And she pointed somewhere behind him, but he wasn't really paying attention.

Marilyn sagged against the reception desk.

'Is there a bar?'

'It's closed now,' said the receptionist. 'No customers.' She had a foreign accent. 'There's a minibar in the room. Or you can have room service.'

They started kissing in the lift. Robert liked the taste of her and slipped his hands under her coat to feel her body. Marilyn's hand brushed against his groin.

'Wasn't this a good idea?' she said.

When they got to the room Marilyn opened the mini-bar. Robert said he didn't want a drink, that he'd had enough. But she didn't take the hint, took out a miniature bottle of wine, unscrewed the cap and emptied it into a glass. He tried to distract her by kicking off his shoes and getting on the bed.

'Come on and try it out,' he said.

She put her drink on the side table and lay beside him. They kissed and Robert fumbled with the zip of her dress. Somehow, Marilyn slipped off the bed onto the floor. She started laughing as she clambered back up. He tried to kiss her again, but her head sagged against the pillow. She'd passed out.

Robert covered her with a blanket he found in the wardrobe. He couldn't sleep and sat up against the headboard with the room lights off, watching television with the sound muted. Switching aimlessly and endlessly between channels he saw a rush of images; riots and girls dancing and men shooting guns and cars crashing and bursting into balls of orange flame. It was like a crazy dream, and he was glad Marilyn was there, lying next to him in the darkened room.

When he woke up the television was still on and a grey light showed through a gap in the curtains. On the other side of the bed the blanket had been pushed aside. Marilyn had gone. He pushed his face into her pillow and inhaled her smell.

*

Robert had screwed a dusting stick to the extension pole and set about clearing away all the cobwebs in the house. He was reaching up into a corner of the living room when his phone rang. It was Marilyn. She was crying.

'Oh, Robert. What must you think of me?'

'You just had a little too much to drink,' he said.

'I don't actually remember what happened,' she said.

'Nothing to worry about.'

'Do you think you could ever forgive me?'

'For what?'

'I don't know,' she paused for what he thought was a long time. 'What happened in the hotel?'

'You went to sleep, that's all.'

'I feel rotten,' she said, and started crying again.

He said she should come over and have dinner and spend the night, but only if she wanted to. And there was a spare bed, anyway.

'That'd be nice,' she said. 'It's meant to be the best way of finding out what a man is like, you know, seeing his home.'

'It's a house,' he said. 'I mean it's not a flat, or anything like that.'

*

Marilyn was a little late because, she said, the cab hadn't come on time. She wheeled an overnight bag into the hallway, handed Robert a bottle of wine wrapped in a twist of white paper, and kissed him on the lips. He took her coat, taking a moment to wonder at how the fabric of her dress strained against her breasts and the roundness of her stomach.

Robert showed her into the living room and mixed them both a gin and tonic. For a moment, before he chinked the glasses together to get her attention, he watched her from behind as she looked up at the photograph of Alison above the fireplace.

'It's in the Hollywood style, as Jean Harlow. I took it myself.'

'She was very voluptuous,' said Marilyn.

'I looked after her right up until the end. But she lost her appetite and wasted away.'

Marilyn was drinking too quickly. He'd expected that because he knew she couldn't help herself. Anyway, it would be better if she got a little drunk. When he saw his own glass was nearly empty, he realised how nervous he was.

He had placed candles all around the dining room, and she said it was so romantic to dine by candlelight. His garlic prawns impressed her and she smiled at him every time he topped up her wine. The lamb was slow roasted. He carved it at the table and brought out more wine, a Sicilian red, and encouraged her to drink it.

'You're a good cook,' she said.

'I enjoy it,' he said. 'It's a hobby, I suppose.'

He had made profiteroles for dessert. She made little noises of pleasure as she ate and he watched her.

'You've hardly touched yours.'

'I don't really like sweet things. And when you're the cook, sometimes, you know, you can't face it.'

Later, when they were in the sitting room having coffee, she kept slumping against the back of the sofa. He was surprised; it had started to take effect much quicker than he thought.

'I feel tired,' she said. 'Really tired.'

He helped her up the stairs into Alison's room, and sat her on the queen-size bed. She was like a puppet with cut strings; arms flopping and head drooping. He lifted her face towards his, kissed her and ran his hand over the swell of her breasts. Then he undressed her and pulled a nightdress over her head. It was new, pink satin, one of Alison's she'd never had a chance to wear.

In the morning Robert gently shook Marilyn awake. She opened her eyes and blinked. For a moment he'd been worried he had been too generous with the dose because he'd overestimated her weight. Wishful thinking, he thought. Now, of course, he would have to be more careful; he didn't want any mistakes.

'How are you this morning?' he said, helping her to sit up and fussing with the pillows behind her.

'I feel awful,' she said, settling back. 'Did I have too much to drink? Again?'

'It's just because you're tired and anxious. Do you know why?' She shook her head. 'Because you haven't been looking after yourself. All those skinny lattes and faddy diets. That's not the sort of person you are. Trying to be someone else, well it's just a strain, isn't it?'

As Marilyn fumbled for her glasses, Robert put a tray with legs down on the bed in front of her.

'What's this?' she said, looking at the cafetiere, the glass of orange juice, the croissant with butter and jam, the pain chocolat, another plate with two cream-filled chocolate éclairs, and a single rose in a small glass vase.

'Breakfast,' he said.

'It looks wonderful.'

Robert sat on the edge of the bed to watch her eat. When she'd finished the croissant and the pain chocolat, he picked up one of the éclairs and guided it towards her lips. 'Open wide,' he said, pleased she opened her mouth without any further prompting. Cream squirted out onto her chin. He wiped it off with a napkin, the way he had in the restaurant, and she smiled at him before taking another bite. And another.

Robert was happy to see her reach for the second éclair of her own volition. It wouldn't do to be pushy. He'd scooped out the original cream and mixed it with a concoction of his own, using extra sweetener to disguise the taste.

'I hope you like this room,' he said.

Her eyes flicked around, taking in the floral patterns on the wallpaper, the curtains, the duvet cover and the carpet. She nodded because her mouth was full.

'I think of it as a beautiful garden. And do you know what the best thing about it is?' She shook her head. 'These flowers will never fade. They'll always be in bloom.'

Marilyn smiled. To Robert she looked literally like the cat that had the cream. But perhaps it was too soon to tell her they were going to live happily ever after.

Cuckoo

Nick had written a eulogy for Robyn. He was going to say she was the kindest person he'd ever known.

Flora was already in the chapel when he arrived. He saw her sitting on the front row, wearing a black wide-brimmed hat, with black velvet roses around the crown. Nick thought it was too theatrical, too demanding of attention.

'Nice hat,' he said, as he sat beside her.

She gave him one of her looks. He glanced at the coffin on the dais and pretended to read the order of service again. Waiting for a funeral to begin was meant to be time to think about the dead. But thinking about Robyn meant thinking about the past. It was like being in Purgatory, he thought, trying to decide whether or not he was a good person.

*

His father had turned up at the school one Saturday morning in the middle of the summer term. Nick didn't know anything about it. He'd been smoking behind the cricket pavilion with Toby Prentiss, who was showing off the flick knife he'd brought back from Spain. Dixon, one of the fourth formers, had been sent to find Nick and send him to the headmaster's study because he had a visitor.

He knocked on old Hale's door and when he was told to come in, he was surprised to see his father sitting there in his civvies; Harris Tweed jacket, cavalry twills and brown suede brogues. The headmaster gave Nick a funny look. He said he was very, very sorry, and that his door was always open. It didn't make sense until they were walking to the car. His father told him his mother was dead.

'Sleeping pills,' he said. 'Booked into a hotel in Scarborough to do it. A bit of a shock for the chambermaid who found her. Bloody typical.'

Everything Nick saw from the car – the fields and the trees at the side of the road – looked normal. They drove to the town and went to a fish and chip restaurant. Nick ate cod and chips. His father had a cup of tea and smoked a cigarette, and said he was being posted to Germany. He wouldn't have a place for Nick to stay until Christmas. 'At the very least.' But he'd find him somewhere for the summer. A billet, he called it, as if it was Nick who was in the army, waiting for a posting.

When he got back to school, he told Toby his mother had died. It got round the others. But like Toby, no one knew what to say. Nick didn't mention it was suicide. Just like he'd never said anything about her being in a psychiatric hospital, because he knew they'd take the piss out of him for being the son of a loony.

His mother's funeral was his first funeral. His father had told him to wear his school uniform because there wasn't time to get him a suit. His mother's neighbours were there. They looked at him. He knew they were trying to look sad, but there was a coldness in their faces that made him feel as if he'd done something wrong.

And when the vicar talked about how his mother would always be in their memories, Nick tried to remember when she was his loving mummy, rather than the angry woman she became. He started to sob. His father put his hand on his shoulder and told him to control himself.

'At least that's over,' his father said, as they drove back to the school. And when they were standing by the car to say goodbye, Nick tried to hug his father. But he pushed him away.

'We'll have none of that,' he said. 'Never wear your heart on your sleeve, Nicky. It gives you away.' He held him by the shoulders and looked into his eyes. 'Never show other people what you're feeling. Do you hear? Always keep that to yourself.'

So Nick never asked about the summer, about where he was going to go. It was Toby Prentiss who told him.

'You're coming to us,' he said. 'It's all arranged.'

Toby had been on the phone to his mother. She'd been for dinner with Nick's father, he said, and they'd fixed the thing up between them. Toby was pleased, and Nick thought he should be too. But how his father and Toby's mother had come together was a mystery.

Toby's parents were getting a divorce, and his father, who was a vet, had moved away. But his mother and sister still lived in Richmond, which was near the Garrison, and Nick began to think his father and Mrs Prentiss must have met at a regimental dance, or something like that.

Everything was confirmed on sports day. Nick won the two-twenty race, and when his father came over to congratulate him, he was with Toby and a blonde woman who turned out to be Toby's mother. She said how much she was looking forward to having Nick stay with them for the summer. Toby said he was too. Nick supposed they would have to become actual friends now, rather than just schoolmates.

On the last day of term Nick and Toby were smoking behind the cricket pavilion. Toby went on about his parents' divorce, and said his mother must have done something wrong for his father to want to leave home.

'I don't think she could have been very nice to him,' he said. 'Otherwise he wouldn't have gone off to live with someone else. He would have stayed. Wouldn't he?'

When Toby asked Nick what it was like when his mother died, he remembered his father's advice. He said it made him feel a bit sad, that's all. But he didn't know what he really felt. His mother had been awful to him after she had what his father called 'a nervous breakdown'. He'd visited her in the psychiatric hospital once. He'd gone alone and the place unnerved him. She seemed to be able to read his mind, and knew he couldn't wait for the visit to end. He was just like his father, she said. 'An absolute shit.'

Of course, he said none of this, and Toby put an arm around his shoulder, a confirmation they were actual friends. The arm felt like an invasion, but given the circumstances, Nick thought it best to go along with the idea.

Mrs Prentiss came to pick the boys up the next day. Nick had expected Toby would be cool towards his mother. Hadn't he blamed her for his father leaving? But they embraced each other, she smoothed his hair back and looked at him. Nick saw the love and admiration in her face. He felt awkward. It was like that moment in the school play when he'd forgotten his lines, while everyone else seemed so sure of theirs.

Mrs Prentiss rescued him, paying him some attention as they loaded their bags into the back of her estate car. She said he should call her Robyn as she wouldn't be able to bear 'Mrs Prentiss this' and 'Mrs Prentiss that' all summer long.

She took her shoes off as she got into the driving seat. 'I like to drive in bare feet,' she said. 'Like Brigitte Bardot.' And as she passed her shoes to Nick, sitting in the back seat, she told him he was very welcome in their house and he was to think of it as his home.

It was a large stone-built bungalow on the outskirts of the town. Toby said it was architect designed, which Nick knew meant it had cost a lot of money. It was certainly different from the army quarters he had been used to and the spartan conditions at the school. The rooms were full of light; an open plan kitchen-dining room, a sitting room with picture windows, views over the lawned garden and the fields beyond. A long corridor led to the bedrooms, and Nick was surprised his room had its own bathroom with a shower.

He described it all in a letter he wrote to his father after he'd arrived. Everything was 'modern and up to date' was how he put it. Nick wanted his father to think he was happy about everything, so he wasn't an annoyance to him.

He met Toby's younger sister, Flora, at lunch that first day. She looked across the table at him as if he wasn't really there, and asked how long he was going to be staying with them. And looking at her mother, she said, 'I mean, hasn't he got a home of his own to go to?' Nick didn't know what to say and stared back at her, trying to appear as if she hadn't been hurtful. He took some consolation in the thought she looked too much like Toby to be pretty. Robyn said she didn't know why Flora was being so rude, she knew Nick was staying with them for the summer.

'Welcome to our broken home,' said Flora.

Toby told Nick to ignore her, and after lunch he said he wanted to show Nick his room. But really he wanted to show off his things; an air rifle with a telescopic sight, the flick knife he was so pleased with, a Pentax camera, a stereo. And an electric guitar, a white Fender Stratocaster.

'Just like the one Jimi Hendrix plays,' he said.

They sat on the bed and he started to play something without the guitar being plugged in. It made a tinny sound and he had to keep stopping to tune it, and then he played the same thing over and over, because he kept making mistakes, and had to start again. It went on for what seemed a long time and Nick didn't recognise the tune, and thought Toby had forgotten he was there.

Nick wanted to be on his own. That summer he was reading a James Bond book, *From Russia with Love*, and he would rather be reading it than have to put up with Toby and his sister.

Outside the sun was shining. The room was hot and smelled the way the dorm did in the mornings, of boys and sleep. Nick was pleased when Toby said they should go for a walk. They headed down the main road towards the town, and after passing a new housing estate, turned onto a track between high hedges that led to another road. They crossed this and went into a wood.

Toby said he was going to show him 'something you're really going to love'. A path ran through the wood along the top of a steep slope above the river. They scrambled down towards a clump of bushes, which concealed a crude hut made of rusting sheets of corrugated iron. They crawled inside and crouched down under the low roof. The floor was a piece of brown linoleum. Dried leaves, and bottles and cans were scattered everywhere. Toby pointed to something, a piece of pink cloth.

'Girl's knickers,' he said. He told Nick some squaddies had built the hut, he called it 'a hovel', as a place to have sex. He said they could bring some dirty mags here and look at them together. 'We could bring girls here too. We could get them to do anything we wanted.'

'How would we do that?'

'Show them this.' Toby had the flick knife in his hand. He pressed the catch, the blade clicked out. There were rumours Toby used it to threaten the younger boys at school into giving him things; money, cigarettes, dirty mags.

'It's stuffy in here,' said Nick, and he crawled out, back into the air. Below him the river rushed over the rocks and through the trees he saw sunlight glittering on the water below.

'I really want to do it this summer. Don't you?' said Toby.

Nick knew he meant sex, and nodded, not wanting to agree to anything out loud. Toby put his arm round him again, to show they were actual friends, as if he needed to confirm it.

After supper they walked into the town. In the market square a group of teenage girls in mini-skirts were bunched up round a bench, smoking. Nick and Toby stared at them. 'You can have your eyeballs back for a shilling,' one of them shouted. The other girls began screeching, and Nick felt their laughter beating around his head.

They were just tarts, dressing like that, said Toby. He led Nick off the square and up a street to The Black Lion. There was a room at the back, a snug, with a bar in the corner, an open fireplace, black beams decorated with horse brasses, and paintings; hunting scenes with horsemen in red coats.

Nobody seemed to care if they were underage or not, and Nick thought their Levi's and cord jackets must have made them look older than they did in their school uniforms. The barmaid was pretty and when Toby ordered their beer, he called her 'princess' and she rolled her eyes at him.

They were both drunk when they left the pub. As they walked back to the bungalow Toby began to go on about the girls who had laughed at them and the pretty barmaid.

'They're all tarts,' he said. 'Aren't they? We should take one or two of them down to the hovel and teach them a lesson. Shouldn't we?'

Nick wasn't really listening. He was too busy walking with his head down, trying to concentrate on his feet because he was so drunk.

When they got back Robyn was in the sitting room drinking gin and smoking. She must have been out somewhere because she was wearing a dress with a pearl necklace and big earrings. She told Toby to get a couple of beers from the fridge because she wanted the boys to sit with her.

'You can only tell what a man's really like when he's drunk,' she said. 'Some men only think about sex. And they think all they have to do is take a woman out for dinner. Think a woman should be only too happy to crawl into the back of their car.' She sat back and took a drag on her cigarette. 'Do you know what the bastard called me tonight?' They both shook their heads. How could they know? 'Miss Frigidaire,' she said, and Nick knew she was drunk. He was surprised because everything about Robyn, the way she dressed and spoke, made her seem so at ease with the world.

In the morning Nick felt groggy. After a shower he went to the kitchen, expecting to find Robyn or Toby, or even Flora. A young woman wearing a light blue overall, the kind they called a tabard, was cleaning something in the sink. She turned and looked at him. There was something hard about her face; sharp cheekbones and fierce make up. She said hello without smiling.

'I'm Nick,' he said.

'I know,' she said. 'Mrs P told me. You're the kid whose mummy died.'

She told Nick to help himself to one of the boxes of cereal on the table. She said she would make him tea or coffee, and cook up some bacon and eggs if he wanted. But first, she was going out for a smoke because it was sunny and it was a shame to waste the weather. Nick was facing the window and saw her appear outside on the patio. She pulled a packet of cigarettes from the pocket of her overall. Over his bowl of cornflakes, he watched her hold her face up to the sun as she smoked.

Toby came in and sat at the table. He saw where Nick was looking.

'That's Janie,' he said. 'She's from the estate. Her Dad works for the gravel company. Drives a wagon. Mum has her in to clean and stuff. She's a bit of a tart, isn't she? Look how short that skirt is.'

'She said she would make bacon and eggs.'

'I wish she would hurry up,' said Toby. 'I'm starving.'

As Janie moved around the kitchen, making tea, frying bacon and eggs, and checking the toast under the grill, they watched her. They had a way of looking at girls and women. Looking and pretending not to look, not sure if they were noticing something they shouldn't. Like the time Marge, the grocer's daughter, had bent into the freezer for a choc ice, and her blouse had parted to reveal a glimpse of white bra.

They were obsessed with sex in the Lower Sixth. But their experience was limited to women like Robyn; the school matron, the school secretary with her Sunbeam Alpine, the Spanish master's wife with her dark hair.

Now, as Janie put a plate down in front of him, Nick caught the smell of her, a sharp smell of sweat, and felt a tremor of excitement. Some secret thing was emanating from her body; something he had to pretend not to notice.

And he spent the following days pretending not to watch Janie as she dragged the Hoover around the house, or when she came into his room with an 'excuse me' to clean the bathroom, leaving her smell to taunt him. And the looks she gave him sometimes. He pretended not to notice those because he didn't understand them.

As the summer stretched on Flora treated him with contempt, making a 'cuckoo' sound to annoy him if her mother wasn't in the room. And he had to go along with whatever Toby wanted to do. To sit in his room as he hunched over his guitar, or wait to be given his turn to shoot tin cans with the air rifle. It was, like Toby's arm around his shoulder, the price he had to pay for somewhere to stay.

In the middle of July, Robyn had to take Toby and Flora to see their father. Robyn told him Janie would make him lunch, and they'd be back that evening. Nick watched them drive away, waving after them from the front door. He was happy to be alone, of not having to spend time with Toby or to put up with Flora's disdain.

After they'd gone, he went out into the garden and sat on a bench with his book. Janie came out. For a smoke, she said. She asked him if he wanted a cigarette, and held out the packet, a filter tip pulled out for him to take. She lit a match and as he leant in to take a light, he felt her fingers brush against his. A shock passed through his skin. Nick didn't know if her touch was deliberate but, like the smell of her body, it felt like something forbidden.

She stood in front of him, cigarette in mouth, and put her hands behind her head to fiddle with her hair. She wore a sleeveless blouse under her tabard, and a thick bush of dark hair showed under each armpit. Nick knew they held the smell of her, the sharp tang of sweat from working in the heat. Women like Robyn shaved their armpits. It wasn't the only thing that set Janie apart. Her make-up was fierce; thick mascara, dark eyebrows, bright turquoise eyeshadow and red lipstick. 'She looks like a tart,' Flora said once, meaning she looked like the girls who hung around with squaddies; the ones who dared Toby and Nick to fancy them.

‘Your Dad?’ said Janie. ‘Where’s your Daddy?’

‘He’s in Germany. In case the Russians attack.’

‘Army, is he? Wasn’t he here once? Seeing Mrs P?’

‘I don’t know. Maybe. To get me a billet.’

‘Is she your new mummy?’

Nick said no as firmly as he could, feeling butterflies in his stomach.

‘That’s right. He’s paying her to look after you. I think she needs the money. Keeps going on about how she might have to sell this house. And then I’ll be out of a job.’

‘Couldn’t you get another one?’

‘There’s always bar work. But you have to put up with men. Gawping and wanting to paw you. I bet that’s what you’re like, too. You’re all like it, and you never grow out of it.’

Nick said he wasn’t like that, but she just laughed.

‘I clean the house. Remember? I’ve seen what you’ve got under your bed.’

She meant the magazine with black and white pictures of women with bare breasts Toby had ‘loaned’ him. Looking at the pictures made his cock go hard and now his face burned. Janie said the women in the photographs were odd because they had nothing ‘down there’. They had no bush, she said. And laughed again because she knew she’d shocked him.

‘Do you like my tabard?’ she said, swinging her hips. ‘Don’t you think it’s sexy?’

Nick laughed to cover his embarrassment. She was wearing a miniskirt and lifted one foot onto the bench. The down on her bare thigh glowed in the sun. It was funny, she didn’t mind him looking. There was a mark on the skin. She wet her finger and rubbed at it.

‘It’s not dirt, you know’ she said. ‘It’s a bruise. How do these things happen, eh?’

Nick didn't know what she meant. Or how to respond. Janie nipped the glowing end off of her cigarette and put it in the pocket of her tabard. She said, 'no rest for the wicked' and he followed her inside, because he sensed she wanted him to.

She went into the sitting room, turning to make sure Nick was watching her. Robyn kept her drinks on a tray on the sideboard. Janie opened one of the bottles and poured herself a glass.

'What are you doing?' said Nick.

'I'm going to have a drink,' she said.

'Should you be doing that?'

'Are you going to stop me?'

Nick shook his head.

'It's a funny thing,' she said. 'Cleaning a house you don't live in. The things you see. Things no one thinks you do. The things you have to clean up. And the things you have to put up with.'

'But it doesn't belong to you.'

'It doesn't belong to you either. But here you are. The lodger.'

Nick took the glass off her and drank from it.

'It tastes like perfume,' he said.

'Gin,' she said. 'Mrs P likes it, doesn't she? Mother's ruin, they call it.'

'Is she sad because of the divorce?'

'You're sad,' she said. 'But I suppose it's because your mummy died.'

'I miss her. The way she was before. But Dad said you mustn't let your feelings get the better of you.'

Janie put her arms around him. He smelled her and she kissed him and he tasted her tongue in his mouth. She led him by the hand to his bedroom and undressed him, and then she showed him the thick bush between her legs, and they lay down on the bed.

The sensation of his skin against hers, and the smell of her, drove him on. Pressure was building in his head and in his cock, and his heart was beating too fast. Janie guided him inside her. She asked him how it felt and he said it felt wonderful.

'That's what it's meant to feel like, darling,' she said and kissed him.

He told Janie he thought she was the most beautiful woman in the world, because that's what James Bond had said to Tatiana Romanova in *From Russia With Love.*

'I love you,' he said.

'It's just a bit of fun,' said Janie. 'Don't take things too seriously.'

She started to get dressed. He wasn't to say anything, she said, because if Mrs P found out, there'd be hell to pay. And then they wouldn't be able to do it again. Nick thought about what his father had said. Perhaps keeping your feelings a secret was the same as keeping something that had happened a secret.

After Janie left, he wandered about the house, thinking about what she had said about him being a lodger. And he knew it was true; he was a stranger in every room. In Toby's room he looked at the guitar on its stand, and started knocking the back of his fingers against the strings, hitting them harder and harder until the skin around his nails started to bleed.

Nick knew there was something wrong when Robyn brought Toby and Flora back. He heard her tell them both to grow up as they came into the house. The thing was, he hadn't wanted to be caught skulking as if he had something to hide, and had gone to the front door to greet them when he heard the car.

'Oh, hello,' said Robyn, as if she was surprised to see him. 'I hope you managed without us.'

Flora looked at him and said, 'I'd forgotten he was here.'

Nick said hello to Toby. He got a hard look back and wondered if they'd been arguing about him. Or if there had been some visible change in him because he'd had sex with Janie. Although it made no sense, he thought it might explain why Toby was standing there with a scowl on his face.

Toby said he'd been cooped up in the car for too long. He wanted to go out. Nick knew it was another thing he had to go along with. As they walked down the drive and along the road, Toby walked with his head down and his fists clenched. He didn't say anything until they turned into the lane leading to the wood.

'My Dad's just told us he's moving to Australia,' he said. 'What do you think of that?'

'Why's he going?'

'There's loads of money to be made out there. They need vets, see? And he's got a new girlfriend and he wants to start a new life.'

Toby went on about how far away it was. Did Nick know how long it took to get there? Nick said he and his mother and father had sailed from Singapore when he was little, and it had taken weeks.

'It's all her fault. My mother's. You betcha. All her fault.'

They crossed the road and went into the wood. Nick knew they were going to the hovel. Toby was behind him on the path, blocking the way back.

'Flora was right about you,' he said. 'You know what she says? You're a cuckoo, come to make a mess of things for us. Always moping about. Always, oh, feel sorry for me, my mummy's dead.'

'I don't. I don't say that.'

'You don't have to say it. It's those puppy dog eyes. Got my Mum round your little finger, haven't you?' Toby moved towards him, fumbling in his pocket, Nick knew, for the flick knife. 'What I want to know is, what's your Father got to do with it? Got to do with my Mum and Dad falling out.'

‘I don’t think he’s got anything to do with it.’

Nick wished he had Bond’s Beretta. That would shut Toby up.

‘So, how did your Dad get my Mum to take you in?’

‘He’s in Germany, Tobes. He’s not here. I don’t know how he met Robyn.’

‘Mrs Prentiss to you,’ said Toby.

He had the knife clear of his pocket now, but his hand was shaking. He was fumbling for the switch to flick the blade out. Nick rushed forward and punched him in the face. Toby lost his balance and fell backwards. Tumbling down the slope, he crashed against a tree, bouncing off it as if he was nothing but a sack filled with straw. He came to rest about thirty feet below the path.

Nick called down to him. But there were only the sounds of the wood; the river flowing over rocks, birds singing, leaves rustling in the breeze. And traffic moving along the road. He remembered the day his father told him his mother was dead. Everything had seemed normal then. Everything seemed normal now. Only Toby lying there and not moving, was odd.

Grabbing hold of branches and roots, Nick made his way down the slope. Toby didn’t say anything when Nick asked him how he was. There was a faraway look in his eyes. He tried to speak, and coughed up a spurt of blood. His eyes changed, and Nick knew he was dead. There was a gnawing in his chest. It wasn’t the thought he’d killed Toby. It was the terror of being found out.

‘Mummy,’ he said, remembering the way she’d comforted him as a child. Like the time she laid her cool hand on his forehead when he had a headache. If only she were here now, he thought, to save him.

But he knew he was on his own. He heard his father’s voice, telling him the need to control himself. Hadn’t he stopped being a boy when he'd done it with Janie? And now he'd killed someone. So what did that make him? He could confess all and face the consequences, or he could live with it, and what had happened would always be his secret.

He found the flick knife on his way back up to the path and put it in his pocket to return to Toby's room later. As he climbed, he made up a story. Toby had wanted to race him through the wood, and as he'd taken the lead, he'd tripped on a tree root, lost his footing and fallen down the slope.

He repeated the story over and over to himself. How Toby had been laughing just before he tripped. How there'd been an awful cracking sound when he hit the tree. In telling it out loud to himself, he stopped to catch his breath at this point, as if he was about to cry. The story and how to tell it was in his mind as he stepped out onto the road and waved down a car. He told it to the woman who was driving, he told it to the police. He was well versed in the telling of it by the time they took him to the Prentiss's bungalow and broke the news to Robyn.

Nick expected her to slap him, to throw him out. But Robyn enveloped him in her arms. The smell of her hair reminded him of his mother and he wept on her shoulder. What did it matter who the tears were really for? Robyn thought they were for Toby.

'He loved you so much and you were his friend,' she said. 'So I love you too.'

He spent the rest of the summer at the bungalow. Robyn smothered him. Mothered him. But Flora still treated him with disdain. Did she suspect he'd killed Toby? That he was a murderer? It was self-defence he told himself, an accident no one would understand. Anyway, nothing could be proved.

Something had changed in him. Janie said he didn't seem so sorry for himself any more. And when he went back to school, the other boys regarded him differently, because he supposed, he'd been in the presence of death.

Robyn wanted him to come for Christmas. Nick's father was pleased because it got him off the hook. His schoolwork had gone downhill since his mother's death, and he'd done badly in his mock A-levels, but Robyn encouraged him, pushing him to get the grades he needed for university. She even came to his graduation and had a framed photograph of him, in his gown and mortar board, on her sideboard.

But there were other changes she had to face. Flora went off to art school and avoided Nick on his visits. Janie left to marry a corporal in the Royal Signals. By then Robyn had been forced to sell the bungalow and move to a smaller house on one of the newer estates.

*

After the funeral they went back to Robyn's house. Nick stood on the other side of the room from the crowd gathered at the buffet table, reflecting on how small this house was compared to the architect designed bungalow where he'd spent that summer. He was looking at his graduation photograph in its gilt frame on the sideboard when Flora came over. She told him he'd made a nice speech.

'I'd forgotten she used to drive in bare feet. How clever of you to remember.' She picked up the photograph. 'Mum used to look at this sometimes and think it was a picture of Toby. Said didn't Toby do well? Sometimes she thought you were Toby, Nick. Did you know that?'

'Yes, I knew,' he said. But he didn't say he never minded, or he sometimes called Robyn 'Mummy'. Flora didn't have to know because it wasn't any of her business. It was a secret.

The Dripping Tap

Helen wasn't happy. It wasn't because she didn't like the restaurant, a converted church on the High Street. It was because Gemma and Tony had been arguing before they'd come out. And now there was an atmosphere, spoiling what she'd hoped to write up in her journal as 'a pleasant evening out with old friends'.

The waitress led them up the staircase to a table on the mezzanine. Tony, without asking the others, or even looking at the wine list, ordered a bottle of Pinot Noir. The starters hadn't arrived before it ran out. He picked up the empty bottle, and waved it at a passing waiter to order another. Gemma said something to him under her breath.

'Don't show me up,' he said.

'You do that all by yourself,' she said. 'You don't need me to do it for you.'

Helen wanted them to stop; they were always like this. She'd hoped it would be different. But Tony was on script, making a point of drinking too much, always reaching for the bottle, in what she regarded as a display of male bravado. Of course,

Robert joined in. It was Saturday night. Why shouldn't they let their hair down?

'We're finally getting the new kitchen fitted next week,' said Helen, realising Gemma would think she was showing off. But she hadn't meant it like that. She just wanted them both to know a house was a home, something to be nurtured so it might nurture them in return.

'Really? Did you hear that, Tony? Helen and Robert are getting their new kitchen…At last.'

'Aren't they the lucky ones?' said Tony, topping up his glass.

'Ours is falling apart,' said Gemma. 'It should be in a kitchen museum.'

'It's perfectly serviceable. There's no point in throwing good money away.'

'It's had its day. It's worn out. And that wretched tap. I can hear it when I'm in bed. It drips all bloody night.'

'Get something from the doctor to help you sleep,' said Tony. 'Or some ear plugs.'

'Fuck off,' said Gemma.

When they'd paid the bill, Helen was the first to her feet. She put on her coat and went downstairs, using the banister rail for support. She watched the others dithering at the top of the stairs. Bored with their slow, drunken progress, she just wanted to go home.

Gemma lost her balance and fell forward. Her body tumbled and crashed all the way down the stairs. Helen rushed over and knelt beside her, shocked at the blood on Gemma's face, at the fact she was unconscious. Not sure what to do, she looked up. Tony was still near the top of the staircase, hanging onto the rail, looking down with his mouth open. Other people, the manager and a woman who said she was a doctor, took control. An ambulance came.

Helen felt a pressure building in her chest all through the taxi ride home. She held onto the feeling as they said goodnight to the babysitter, and kept it inside her as she checked on the boys asleep in their beds. It wasn't until she came back downstairs, and was finally alone with Robert, that she was able to let it out.

'He tripped her,' she said. 'I saw him trip her.'

'What are you talking about?'

'Tony tripped Gemma up. Deliberately.'

But Robert wasn't listening; he was looking for something amongst the bottles on the sideboard.

'Do you want a brandy?' he said.

'Do you really need another drink?'

'Don't you start…'

'Pour one for me then,' she said. 'And listen. For God's sake. Just listen.'

'You need to calm down,' said Robert, handing her a brandy.

'For fuck's sake, Robert. I wasn't that drunk. I know what I saw.'

'You're overreacting, because you're pissed, Helen.'

'I witnessed a criminal assault, for God's sake.'

'Get a grip, woman. You're being ridiculous. Gemma was pissed. She lost her balance. It was an accident.'

'You don't think I should go to the police?'

'What? Report one of our friends to the police? It's not the sort of thing people like us do, is it?'

'Oh, I don't know,' said Helen. 'It is if they've done something wrong.'

Robert told her to forget all about it. But she couldn't. The more she thought about it, the more she was possessed by the same internal pressure she'd felt in the taxi. In the morning she made Robert phone Tony to find out what had happened to Gemma.

She'd regained consciousness and was still in the infirmary. They were keeping her in for observation.

After breakfast, Helen left Robert reading the Sunday papers, and drove round to see Tony. He looked awful, hung-over and unshaven. Despite the autumn chill he was wearing shorts, and a faded t-shirt that hung over his gut like a tent. Gemma was still in the hospital, he said. He didn't know when she was coming home, and he couldn't make her any coffee because he'd turned off the water at the mains.

Helen followed him down the hallway into the kitchen. There was a toolbox on the breakfast bar, and tools on the worktop by the sink. He'd taken the tap apart; bits of it lay on the draining board.

'How is she?' she said. 'Is it serious?'

'Couple of broken ribs, face bashed up a bit,' he said, touching his cheek. 'I don't know. They've got to do some scans, x-rays. I don't know. Things like that.'

'I saw what you did, Tony.'

'What do you mean, you saw what I did? What did I do?'

'I saw you trip Gemma up. You might as well have pushed her down those stairs.'

'She tripped and fell, Helen.'

'I saw you. I saw what you did.'

He picked up a wrench and stood with his back to the sink, staring at her.

'What does Robert think about this?' he said.

'He knows I'm here,' she said.

'What's that meant to mean?'

Tony threw down the wrench. It clattered into the stainless-steel sink. He put his hands against the worktop, lowered his head and sighed.

'We'd all had too much to drink, Helen,' he said, glancing back at her. 'What kind of person do you think I am?'

'I know what I saw, Tony.'

'You didn't see what you thought you saw. I don't know what you're up to, Helen. Are you that bored? Do you need the attention? Is that what this is about?'

'I wanted to see what you'd say about it.'

'Nothing,' he said. 'I've got nothing to say about it. Because it didn't happen. Alright?'

'I'm going to see Gemma, Tony. And then I'll decide.'

'Decide what, exactly?'

'Whether or not to go to the police.'

'Get out,' he said, turning to face her.

The bulk of him intimidated her, but she took her time and walked slowly to the front door. As she opened it, she turned to look back at him. He'd picked up the wrench again, and was hefting the weight of it in his hand as if it were a club.

*

The ward was on the third floor. At the nurses' station they directed Helen to the bay, and she stood in the entrance and scanned each bed. At first, she didn't recognise Gemma. Her face was a mass of purple bruising. One of her eyes was swollen half shut. Helen didn't want to show how shocked she was. She tried to soften her expression, and sat down on a red plastic chair next to the bed.

'Helen?' said Gemma. Her voice sounded far away.

Helen took her hand and forced a smile. Gemma was her best friend; they'd met at university. Helen had never liked Tony, but when she met Robert the four of them drifted into the sort of relationship couples have; dinner parties, nights out to the theatre, walks in the country.

Seeing Gemma's injuries made her realise the feeling she hadn't been able to shake since the restaurant was anger. Pure and simple. Hadn't she always thought of Tony as a bully? Gemma was too drugged up, too much in shock for Helen to tell her she'd seen what had happened. The phrase, 'criminal assault' came into her mind again. She ought to report it to the police; it was her duty.

*

Helen had never been into a police station as far as she could remember. She expected an avuncular desk sergeant because that's what they were like on TV. But there was no one. She'd walked into a small entrance lobby lined with dark wood veneer. Worn and scratched, it smelled of some kind of disinfectant; pine-scented, she thought. There was a row of seats fixed to the wall, and a glazed counter like those they have in post offices. She stood, not knowing what to do, until she saw the bell push and the small printed notice; 'Press and Wait'. She pressed the button. A buzzer sounded far away.

Helen wasn't sure if the dishevelled woman who eventually appeared behind the counter was a policewoman or not. She wore a black fleece jacket with the police logo on the chest, and an identity card on a lanyard, but she looked old and tired. A pair of reading glasses hung from a cord around her neck, and her A4 notepad had had several pages ripped out of it.

'Can I help you?'

'I want to report an assault.'

'Name?' said the woman, clicking her ballpoint pen.

'It's not me who's been assaulted. I just saw it happen.'

'I need your name. And your address.'

'Can't I just tell someone what I saw? I know who did it.'

'I need your details.'

Helen wanted to tell her story, but it had taken all her conviction to walk through the door, to get this far. And now she had to give her details, which meant her personal feelings were open to official scrutiny.

The woman told her to take a seat. 'Someone will be out, shortly,' she said.

After another wait, a young woman in a navy trouser suit came out. She said she was a detective constable and showed Helen into an interview room off the lobby. They sat at a bare table on plastic chairs. The detective took notes while Helen told her story. The simple fact, that Tony had tripped Gemma up on the stairs at the restaurant, seemed banal. When she said it out loud it began to sound less real. Less convincing. And there was that question to catch her out.

'Had you been drinking?' said the policewoman.

'We'd all been drinking,' said Helen, and she flushed.

She read the statement the detective had written out for her. It was Helen's story, the basic story of how she'd seen Tony kick out his foot to trip Gemma up. But it wasn't in her own words. There was no emotion in it, nor did it express how awful it had been to hear Gemma's body hitting against the wooden stairs as she fell. 'Like bones cracking,' she'd said, and she'd tried to describe Gemma's face to the detective. But none of this was in the statement she had to sign. It was as if what she'd said had been badly translated from another language.

'You should go to the hospital and see her,' said Helen. 'Then you'd know.'

*

'You're a bloody fool,' said Robert.

He was in a mood about it. He'd warned her against going to the police. Nothing would come of it. Gemma would deny it, and it would just make Helen look stupid or vindictive. It would make fools of them both, he said. It would be the end of their friendship.

Helen couldn't concentrate at work. When people asked what kind of weekend she'd had, she didn't say anything about what had really happened in the restaurant. 'We had a pleasant evening out with old friends,' she said. But she hated lying, and thought she wasn't just trying to hide things from other people, but from herself as well. Saying she felt out of sorts, she left the office in the middle of the afternoon.

She went to the hospital. Gemma didn't look much better, but her voice didn't sound so far away anymore.

'The police have been to see me,' she said. 'A woman detective. What were you thinking, Helen?'

'I saw him trip you.'

'No, you didn't.'

'I know what I saw.'

'You were drunk,' said Gemma. 'You don't know anything.'

'It was criminal assault. He meant to hurt you. What did you say? What did you tell the detective?'

'That I tripped because I'd had too much to drink. I told them Tony and I don't have that kind of relationship. I told them you were drunk too. That you couldn't have seen what you said you'd seen. Because it didn't happen.'

'You know what happened. He could have killed you.'

'Tony might have been sent to prison. Or he could've lost his job. Maybe he'd never get a job again. What good would that do?'

'What are you going to do? Just forget about it? You should leave him.'

'You don't understand. You can't just leave people.'

'Can't you? I thought that's exactly what people did when they weren't happy.'

'Why don't you leave Robert then? If it's that easy, why don't you do it?'

'Why would I do that?'

'Oh, come on. You put on a good act. But you can't fool me with all the happy family stuff. But you know that. And I know you. Remember?'

The blood rushed to Helen's face. There was a hollow feeling in her stomach, and a familiar tingling in her arms and legs. She stood and walked out of the bay, past the nurses' station and out of the ward. In the main corridor she kept walking. She didn't feel the way she worked so hard to feel, even her expensive wool coat was inadequate armour now, and she didn't want anyone guessing how she really felt. She went into the first toilet she saw. As soon as she locked the door of the cubicle she began to sob. There was nothing any different about it; she always cried alone.

It was dark when she left the hospital, and the streetlamps showed wet leaves lying in drifts along the pavement. She had parked on one of the streets behind the university and walked quickly. Anxiety sharpened her senses: she was aware of the drops of water glistening on the roofs of parked cars, the sharp chill in the air, and the sound of traffic from the central motorway. There was something else, another set of footsteps behind her. She was being followed.

Helen knew it was Tony. He must have seen her leaving the hospital on his way to visit Gemma, or perhaps he'd been lying in wait, knowing she'd show up eventually. If he had a chance before she got to the car, he would do something, catch her and beat her up, or worse. She quickened her pace.

The car was parked two or three streets away, too far away for her to outrun him, and even then, she would have to fumble for the car keys in her handbag before she could open the door. The university library was nearer. She walked to the corner and saw the brightly lit entrance on the other side of the covered footbridge over the motorway. She began to run towards the bridge, and her footsteps echoed as she ran through it. There were people now, students with rucksacks and cycles, milling around the building. The glass doors opened automatically and she stepped into the lobby. Warm air rushed against her cold skin. The doors closed behind her and catching her breath, she turned.

Tony was standing at the edge of the light radiating out from the building. He raised his arm as if in greeting. Helen saw her reflection in the glass wave back at him; as if she and her reflection were different people and she and Tony were still friends.

She waited in the lobby, long after he'd slipped back into the darkness, and knew nothing would happen now. When she and Robert saw Gemma and Tony at a party or a gallery opening, they would politely ignore each other. But the thing would still be there. It could never go away, and like Gemma, they would pretend it had never happened. Eventually the story would slip out in the way gossip does, and become one of those unsubstantiated rumours that enliven dinner parties when people are too drunk or too bored to care what they say.

Bright Blue Sky

Spring was Jane's favourite time of year. Out with her walking group on Wednesday, she had seen snowdrops in the woods, and daffodil shoots pushing up through the soil, she wrote in her journal, like fat green fingers.

This morning the sun was shining. From the kitchen window she watched sparrows fluttering in and out of the copper beech hedge. Winter's over, she thought, humming to herself as she made breakfast. The eggs came up to the boil, knocking against each other in the pan, and the kettle began to whistle on the hob, making it difficult to hear the current affairs programme on the radio.

Martin, who was sitting at the kitchen table, made a performance of standing up and muttering as he reached for the volume control. Since retirement he'd become something of a news junkie. Being informed, he called it.

'The lying bastard,' he shouted quite suddenly. 'Don't you think so?'

'I wasn't really listening,' said Jane, trying to remember how many minutes the eggs had been boiling.

'Well, I'm not surprised with all that racket.'

On the radio the presenter and the government minister began to talk over each other.

'See?' said Martin. 'He won't answer the bloody question.'

'Obviously not,' said Jane, disappointed because the yolk of her egg was hard.

Afterwards, she cleared the table and loaded the dishwasher, clattering the crockery into the racks and the cutlery into the basket. She slammed the door shut and switched the machine on. Water rushed into it and Martin turned up the radio again. 'Will you empty it when it's finished?' she said. 'I've got Pilates.'

Martin put a finger to his lips and made a shushing sound.

*

'If he did something about any of it, I wouldn't mind,' she said to Margot when she went round for coffee. 'He could volunteer for something, but he just rants about everything.'

'You need to develop a new interest together. Something you can share.' Margot was looking out of the kitchen window watching Rob, her husband, being chased around the lawn by their new puppy. She laughed. 'Oh, look at that,' she said.

Jane made her best stab at a smile. She had just seen the dog's toy, a yellow rubber chicken lying under the table, an ugly, mutated thing.

'A trip,' said Margot. 'How about a trip? Get to know each other again. Things you've forgotten.'

*

'Brussels?' said Paul, when he and Jane went for their usual coffee after the Thursday literature class. 'Why Brussels?'

'There's a big military museum, apparently,' she said. 'Martin's keen on the Napoleonic Wars and gourmet beer. And he has an urge to see the European Parliament, even though he's a Eurosceptic.' She stopped for breath. 'Is it really that bad?'

'Well , I suppose there's Le Musee des Beaux Arts. It does have some wonderful paintings,' he said. 'There's Brueghel's *Landscape with The Fall of Icarus*, for instance. It's a must see.'

Paul, Jane thought, would have made a better companion for a cultural getaway. She had actually wanted to go to Rome. But Martin had been unenthusiastic, to the point of an absolute refusal.

*

Their hotel was near the European Parliament and they spent a dull hour walking around the precinct, unable to gain access to the visitor centre, because it closed early on a Friday afternoon. 'Bloody EU,' said Martin. They sat outside a café and watched a demonstration in the middle of a roundabout, people wearing anoraks and carrying banners. One read, *Change Europe, Vote Green*. Jane had a hot chocolate, which was tepid and thin and Martin had a beer, one of the many he was to try that weekend.

Back in their hotel room he started to make a fuss because the bookmark had fallen out of his Sharpe novel, disappeared actually, and he had lost his place. Jane looked up from her Kindle; she was rereading *Middlemarch*, and watched as he flicked the pages of the book backwards and forwards.

'Aren't they all the same anyway?' she said.

'What do you mean?'

'I mean, does it really matter?'

He went into a sulk and didn't speak until they began to get ready for dinner. Jane had found a restaurant in the Grand Place on TripAdvisor. It was in a cellar and they both had stoemp, which she didn't like; too grim, like peasant food. She had a half bottle of a reasonable red though, and Martin had three different beers. He became quite garrulous, trying to explain the lead up to the First World War in ludicrous detail. Unfortunately, he had all the facts but no sense of narrative. She looked over his shoulder at the waitress and asked for the bill.

Later they went to an Art Deco bar Jane had read about in the guidebook. She had a cognac and tried to interest Martin in admiring the décor, but he began to mount a defence of Bernard Cornwell's novels to an imaginary critic, she realised it was her, and drank two more beers.

On Saturday morning, Martin lost his reading glasses. She helped him search the room and watched as he searched it again and again. On their way to the Metro they went to a pharmacy to try to find a replacement. Jane watched him spinning the spectacle display, trying a pair on, holding the guidebook at arm's length to test them, and putting them back.

'I need a prescription pair,' he said, after the third attempt. 'Not one off the shelf.'

Jane feigned sympathy, but she became more and more irritated with Martin that day. First, there was Le Musee Royal de l'Armee, where she had to endure not just the endless displays of armour and weaponry, but his lecture on the difference between a rifle and a musket as well. And then there was his complete lack of enthusiasm as they walked around Le Musee des Beaux Arts.

'Isn't it fabulous?' she said, when she found the Brueghel. She looked at the painting; the ploughman, the shepherd looking skyward, the ship with its billowing sail, the sea and land beyond.

'Where's Icarus?' said Martin, scanning it quickly.

Jane pointed out the legs disappearing into the sea.

'Is that it?' he said.

'No one's noticed,' she said.

'Who cares?'

On Monday morning, while Martin queued at hotel reception to pay, Jane wheeled her case outside to wait on the pavement. She stood over a grating in the gutter and looked at the leaves and cigarette ends floating on the dark water below. Glancing from side to side, she took Martin's reading glasses from her handbag, squatted down and dropped them through the grille.

Jane didn't feel guilty. In fact, she didn't understand what she had begun to feel since she had taken the bookmark from his stupid novel and seen the effect. Watching him search for his reading glasses, while pretending to help him look for them, had only increased the sensation.

Back home, Martin began to lose other things. His fountain pen disappeared, the one with green ink that he used to make notes about the Napoleonic Wars. He looked everywhere, for nearly the whole afternoon, and became quite distraught.

'Have you checked down the back of the sofa?' Jane suggested, knowing full well that he had; she'd seen him do it.

She watched again as he ran his hand along the back of the cushions and turned, frustrated, towards her, shaking his head.

'Where the hell is it?' he said, again. The look on Martin's face, bright red and fearful, gave Jane that delicious feeling again.

'Here, let me look,' she said, making a big show of searching, palming the pen from her sleeve and holding it up. 'There. You just weren't looking properly.'

Then Jane put his car keys in the pocket of a jacket he hadn't worn for weeks.

'Have you checked all your coat pockets?' she said, and eventually stood over him whilst he went through the pockets of every coat and jacket in the downstairs cloakroom until there was only one left.

'This is ridiculous,' he said. 'I haven't worn this since...'

'Just check it,' she said.

He put his hand into one of the pockets and pulled out the keys, a bewildered expression on his face. It made Jane think she ought to stop. But the next day the urge just came upon her, and almost as if she were in a trance, she went straight to the chest of drawers in the bedroom where she'd seen his wallet that morning.

She put it in a pair of jeans that he'd left lying on the bedroom floor, and stuffed them to the bottom of the linen basket, under towels and socks and underwear. He never thought to look there, she certainly never suggested it, and in a panic, he cancelled all his cards. When he'd put the phone down after talking to Barclaycard, she came in from the utility room, where she had been loading the washing machine, holding the jeans in one hand and the wallet in the other.

Lucy came home for the weekend, and Jane made a point of confiding in her about Martin's forgetfulness.

'I'm worried about your father,' she said. 'I don't know how to bring it up, but I think he should have a test.'

'What kind of test?'

'Oh, perhaps it's nothing,' she said, turning to look out of the window at a blackbird pecking on the lawn.

'You're over-reacting, mum. He's just adjusting to retirement. I mean he did have a pretty full-on job.'

'Oh, yes,' she said. 'I'm sure you're right.'

Jane didn't actually have a plan; she just kept falling prey to temptation. Martin had left his laptop open and, while he was rooting about in the garage, she changed his password. Not into anything very different, but enough, certainly enough to make him doubt his sanity. She changed *sharpesrifles*, all lower case, to *SHARPESRIFLES*, all upper case, and logged out.

'Are you sure that it's all lower case?' she asked him as he swore in frustration. 'Are you absolutely sure?'

'You can try if you're so bloody clever,' he said.

After her fingers tapped at the keyboard and the start-up chime sounded, he shook his head in disbelief, his mouth gaping open.

'What the…?'

'All upper case,' she said. 'What else could it be?'

Her most imaginative project involved his mobile phone. She began to hide it in the most obscure places; the car boot, under the bed in the spare room, the bottom drawer of his desk. He was forced to locate it by dialling it from the cordless house phone, and run around, receiver in hand, up the stairs and down again, trying to identify where the ringtone was coming from, before the voicemail picked up. If he hadn't found it by then, he had to redial and set off on another frantic search.

Thinking of new places became the challenge. She baulked at the fridge because it seemed too extreme, too unlikely. But it was beckoning; she just lacked the courage. In the end she decided to hide it under the kitchen sink. Martin had been drinking; two gin and tonics before dinner and a shared bottle of wine with the meal. He was on his second brandy, and dozing in front of the television. The impulse came upon her when his head dropped forward and he began to snore. She picked up his phone from the coffee table and went quickly into the kitchen.

Jane was on her knees in front of the cupboard under the sink, her head in the door, holding Martin's mobile as far back as she could reach, beyond the u-bend and the more obscure cleaning products. The phone in her hand began to ring and she jerked back in surprise and hit her head, but she had the good sense to turn around and stand up. Martin was in the doorway.

'What on earth?' he said, holding the house phone up and shaking it. 'I knew something was going on.'

He charged, just as the voicemail on his mobile picked up. '…I can't take your call right now…' Martin made sounds that weren't words, as he came at her. But thanks to her excellent flexibility, her Pilates instructor had only recently commented upon it, Jane glided out of his path.

Martin kept staggering forward and tripped. Jane heard the crack of his head against the granite worktop, and watched her husband collapse to the floor. She stood over him, heard his voice from the handset, '…please leave your message after the tone…' and crouched down at the beep. His eyes were open but unseeing. There was blood too, a dark pool spreading across the terracotta tiles. Signs, she knew, from the crime dramas they watched on TV, that he was dead.

*

'He never really adjusted to retirement. Could never establish a proper routine. And then he started drinking, and forgetting things. I just didn't think he'd try to take it out on me. The attack, well it just came out of the blue, and then he tripped and fell. It was a tragic, tragic accident.' That was what she said to the police, to Lucy and then, dressed in sombre black, to the coroner.

It was what she said to Paul just before the literature class started, the first she'd been to for weeks. They sat together and she felt his eyes on her, and when she turned towards him, she saw the concern in his face. Afterwards, they went to *The Happy Campus Coffee Shop* in the university precinct. The sun was shining and they took a table by the window.

'Poor you,' he said, placing her coffee down in front of her. 'So unexpected. How are you bearing up?'

'It hasn't been easy,' she said, looking down and then up at him. 'Lucy's in bits, as you might expect. The worst thing is…I actually thought that he was going to…'

'Oh my god,' said Paul. 'Do you mean…?'

'I still can't actually say it out loud,' she said, spooning a little of the froth from her cappuccino and tasting it. 'I'm renting a flat until the house is sold. I just can't live there anymore.'

'You should go on a trip. Get a fresh perspective on things.'

'It all started when we went to Brussels, you know.'

'But that wasn't your idea, was it?'

'No. I'd actually wanted to go to Rome.'

'Ah, the Eternal City,' said Paul, smiling at her. 'So much to see.'

Jane felt his fingers brush against hers, and turned to the window as she caught her breath. Looking up she saw a seagull wheel and turn above the quad. She squeezed Paul's hand and watched the bird floating, its white wings outstretched against the bright blue sky.

Boy Saved from Drowning

My sister saved me from drowning. It's the great dinner party story I never tell. But the family talked about it all the time when I was a boy. In the end I never knew how much of it I remembered for myself.

It happened at a bend in the river where families from the village went to swim and picnic in the summer. The older boys lit fires for the fun of it, and wood smoke mixed with the smell of burning fat, spitting from the sausages they held over the flames on sharpened sticks.

There was a meadow and a shingle beach and shallow water. But the river was wide and below the high bank on the other side was a deep pool, good for swimming and diving. Toddlers like me were meant to stay in the shallows. But I must have had the idea to cross over to where the older kids were changing into swimsuits under towels, getting ready to jump in. I was too far out before Mum or Jan noticed where I was.

I'd paddled across, until I must have realized there was nothing under my feet. Water stung my eyes, blurring the light as I thrashed and panicked. This part of it is my own memory, an image triggered now by the sound of children laughing and splashing about in swimming pools, or the smell of summer barbeques.

Isabel, who pinched me to make me cry when our mother wasn't looking, stood high up on the far bank; haughty, slim-hipped and ten years old. The way it was told, she saw what was happening, unzipped her skirt, stepping out of it as she sprinted to the edge and jumped in, feet first. She brought me to the surface and back into the shallows, carrying me, spluttering and bawling, to the grass bank. Sitting with me in her arms, she held me close and kissed my head.

'Oh, Peter Rabbit,' she said. 'What a fright you gave me.'

In giving me that name I was forgiven for taking her place as the youngest child. Now I was beloved. And here is the memory of it, knocking on my door again.

The daffodils were out, showing bright yellow in the park and on the grass verges of the city. Seeing them should have put a spring in my step, but all they did was remind me what time of year it was. I was expecting Jan to call.

I tried to sound indifferent when I answered the phone, to show her how I felt. The problem was we didn't know how to say what we needed to say to each other. I wanted to say what do you want? But I knew what she wanted.

'When are you coming?' she said.

It was what we thought of as 'the anniversary', but we never said it out loud. We knew it wasn't the right word because there was nothing to celebrate. Martin and I would wear our dark suits, Jan a black dress. We'd stand in the cemetery, and stare at the grave, not knowing what to say, and not knowing what else there was to do. Afterwards we would go to the pub, and drink too much as if it were a wake. I didn't know how to get out of it, or even if I really wanted to. But I tried.

'I don't know if I can make it this time, Jan.'

'Please Peter,' she said, and then, 'Please Peter...Peter Rabbit.'

Hearing the name squeezed a gasp out of me, and I heard an echo of it coming back through the ether.

'You'll have to pick me up at Darlington Station,' I said. 'I can't face the drive.'

But I should have driven. There's too much time to think on a train, with nothing to do but look out of the window. The train headed north out of King's Cross, passing the brick terraces, the factories and the industrial estates. In between the towns and cities, were fields of grazing sheep and cattle, and the spires of village churches in the distance. And at the edge of places, the new housing estates. I thought about the families in those houses and how they lived, and how like or unlike my own they were.

A memory of Izzy: I am sitting on her bed and she is twirling around and around in a new dress. She sprays perfume on herself and tells me to smell it. I grab her hand and push my nose against the inside of her wrist.

'It's French perfume,' she says. 'Ooh-la-la.'

The Dansette clicks as another record drops from the stack onto the turntable. The arm moves and drops into the grooves. A hiss and a crackle and Chubby Checker is singing 'Let's Twist Again'. She starts to dance, twisting her feet and moving her arms backwards and forwards, her elbows jabbing the air behind her. Bending her knees, she drops nearer to the floor. Still twisting her feet, she rises back up, moving in time with the music.

'Come on,' she says, 'dance like me. Do what I'm doing.'

I jump up and follow her moves, dancing beside her and then facing her and we are both laughing. I am so happy and Chubby Checker is singing, 'Like we did last summer...'

*

Jan met me at the station barrier.

'I don't know why you couldn't have driven,' she said, but she looked tired and gaunt, so I didn't start a fight.

We drove out through the old pit villages. Some were just a couple of terraces, and others had wide streets and boarded up pubs. We came over the moors. In the distance a line of white wind turbines, their giant blades slowly turning, stretched along the horizon. We dropped down into the valley and on, into the village.

When Mum had died, Jan had moved back to live in our old house. It had been left to us all, but Jan had managed to claim it. 'It's your home, too,' she'd said. 'There's no rush to sell it.' She moved here from Leicester where she'd ended up, and came here with her daughter. She had a failed marriage behind her. Me too. Our brother Martin, who still lived in the village was the same. None of us were any good at relationships.

The house was stone built, an old schoolmaster's house set back from the road behind a high beech hedge. We walked straight into the kitchen and even though Jan had redecorated, the dresser and the big oak table, once the centre of the house, were still there.

'It always smells the same,' I said.

'It's the Aga,' she said. 'We're lumbered with it.'

Lucy was sitting at the kitchen table working the keypad on her phone. Her hair was dyed pink and a paperback copy of Shakespeare's *Romeo and Juliet* lay unopened in front of her. She looked up at me.

'Hi, Uncle Peter.'

There was something awkward about her, which made me feel awkward too, and I gave her a quick hug and a kiss on the cheek.

'How's Romeo and Juliet?'

'It's just for my A Level,' she said, and went back to her phone.

I took my bag upstairs and went to look in Izzy's old room, wanting to see the records she'd left all over the floor, the lid on the Dansette up and the turntable spinning, and to hear music charging the air. I wanted to see her dancing. But the room isn't how it used to be. It's Lucy's room now, with posters of people I don't recognise on the wall, soft toy animals piled up on the bed and a pink laptop on an Ikea desk.

I shouted down I was going to have a bath and filled the tub. The bathroom still had no shower and the chrome taps had brass showing through. The room became dense with steam and I got into the bath, lying back to let the hot water warm me through.

I remembered Izzy bathing me once. She'd opened the window and sat on the old cork topped stool and smoked a cigarette while I splashed around. And, with the cigarette still hanging from the corner of her mouth, she squeezed a flannel of soapy water over my head, and I'd begun to laugh uncontrollably. When she dried me, rubbing me down with the towel, I fell against her and she hugged me and kissed my head.

It was more of a dream than a memory. The hot bath had put me in a faint and I came round not knowing where I was. The steam had cleared and the water was quite cold, but I could smell cigarette smoke and perfume lingering in the air. The impossibility of it sent me clambering out of the bath. I dried myself in a hurry, pulled on my clothes and staggered out onto the landing. I sniffed the air. Nothing.

Lucy was standing in the doorway of her room. I suppose she must have heard me lumbering about.

'Have you been smoking?' I said.

'I don't smoke,' she said and slipped back into her room, closing the door hard behind her. I must have looked quite mad standing there, half-dressed and dripping wet.

*

Memories come unbidden, prompted by what? Proust had his cakes. I had this house and the smell of perfume and cigarettes. And now I remember the afternoon Izzy's breath smelled the same as the breath of the men; uncles, cousins and neighbours, who came to the house at Christmas. They would drink beer and whisky with Dad, smoke and laugh out loud and give us kids ten-shilling notes. And I started to notice, as I got old enough to notice, that some of them would let their hand linger on her waist, or squeeze her a little tighter when they kissed her cheek. I used to think it was because everybody loved her.

We were lying on her bed, she had her arm around me, and Dusty Springfield was on the Dansette singing 'I Just Don't Know What to do With Myself.' Izzy had been crying and her eye make-up, which had been dark like Dusty's, was all blurred. She put on a pair of sunglasses and lit a cigarette.

She tried to laugh, but black tears still rolled out from under the dark lenses.

'Will you always love me?'

'Yes,' I said.

'You must still love me, even when I've gone,' she said. 'I'm going to London.' But then, she was always saying that.

'Yes, Izzy I will love you forever and ever.'

But I didn't ever want her to leave. Not ever.

*

After breakfast the next day, Martin drove up to the house in his Land Rover. He came into the kitchen, his black Labrador Clint behind him, and put a box of vegetables on the table. He had a smallholding where he kept chickens and grew vegetables, but in one of those contradictions of country life, he lived in a modern house on a small estate at the edge of the village.

'There's eggs in there too, Jan,' he said, and turned to me. 'How's London?'

'Still the same,' I said.

'You'll need a walk then.'

We drove out of the village, the dog lying across my lap, until we came to the old quarry, a great cut in the land. We came here as kids in all kinds of weather, and today heavy clouds gave it a melancholy air. We knew the rain would probably catch us but we started to walk anyway. The dog roamed ahead and came back, nuzzling up to one or the other of us and then, finding a new scent, striking out again.

For an hour or more we walked uphill, and skirted the edge of the valley, curving round so when we came down, we could follow the river back to the quarry. I had memories of everywhere we went, and we stopped at the bend in the river where Izzy had saved me from drowning on that bright summer's day. But the sky was dark now, and the wind was pushing ripples across the surface.

The rain caught us and we ran for the wood and the shelter of the trees. We stood with our anorak hoods up, silently waiting for the rain to blow over. Cold and wet, I thought of the kitchen and its fuggy warmth and the smell of old cooking. If it seemed a comfort, I also sensed its confinement and the impossibility of escape. Water dripped from leaves and branches, and the tree trunks glistened wet, like the bodies of giant lizards.

'You were Izzy's favourite,' Martin said. 'But everybody loved her. Not just you.' He crouched down and stroked the dog, which wagged its tail and wriggled at his touch.

As soon as Martin engaged first gear and pulled away from the quarry I knew where we were going. I think I willed him to drive there, but it might have been his idea. We drove down the valley to where it widened out into fields of pasture, coming along narrow winding roads hemmed in by ancient hedgerows. We crossed a small hump backed bridge. It was near a gate, and there was a place where a car could pull in. Martin parked the Land Rover and turned the engine off. We sat in silence.

*

Another visitation: it had been a bright spring day, but the light has faded to a soft haze. I am sitting on the kerb for no reason, and my attention is drawn to the car; a pale blue Ford Zephyr parked at the bus stop. It is facing away from me with its engine running, the exhaust pipe trembling.

I hear footsteps and turn to see Izzy, in her new dress, white with orange spots, and a short suede jacket around her shoulders. She carries her handbag in one hand, a cigarette in the other, and she walks quickly, her high heels tapping on the road. The colours of her dress seem too bright against the grey stone of the houses and the green grass of the hills beyond the village.

'I hope you're not spying on me, Peter,' she says. 'Go home, and don't you dare say a word.'

Izzy doesn't seem like my sister, something about her is different. She gets into the car, slamming the door, and it drives off.

*

Martin got out of the Land Rover and I followed. We climbed the gate. The pillbox had been built to guard the bridge, but the hedgerow had grown back long ago, and now it was hidden from the road. Patches of dark green moss and bright spots of lichen covered the grey concrete. The entrance was down a narrow passage and inside light came through the gun slits and onto the firing platforms.

We stood there in the damp half-light. The pillbox stank of stale piss. The floor was mud now, strewn with rocks and empty beer cans. There were the remains of a fire and an old pair of tights. It was where they had found her body on the second day of the search.

I moved, wanting to leave, and the light caught the texture of the abandoned tights in the dirt. Izzy had been strangled with her own tights. I felt a physical connection to the memory of her, and the cold fact of her death hit me, in that forlorn place where her beautiful body had been abandoned.

I bounced off the edges of the opening and the walls of the passage in my hurry to get out, and vomited onto the grass. Martin came behind me. He touched me on the arm and pressed a cotton handkerchief into my hand. He was older than me, always distant and laconic, but his arm came around my shoulder and he held me while I wept.

I wiped my mouth and took deep breaths of clean air. I smelled the sweet odour of perfume and the tang of tobacco smoke.

'Do you smell anything?' I asked.

Martin sniffed the air. He shrugged, and I let it go.

When I got back to the house Jan was at the kitchen table, looking through some papers. She gathered them up as I came in and slipped them into a folder. Something she didn't want me to see so I didn't ask. She was drinking wine, an Australian Shiraz, and told me to fetch a glass.

'No point in drinking alone,' she said.

I took a glass from the draining board and sat at the table. Jan poured me some wine. She looked tired, worn out with something.

'Why did you come back here?' I said.

'It wasn't just about Izzy, you know. There are other memories. I felt lonely after the divorce, I thought coming back would take the fear out of it.'

'When Izzy died, it didn't seem as if there was any love left in the house anymore.'

'It was what killed Mum,' she said. 'You were too young, I think, to know. You were, what? Nine or ten? And afterwards. I was a good sister to you, wasn't I?'

Jan reached across the table for my hand but I pulled it away.

'I saw the car,' I said. 'And I saw Izzy get into the car. And I can't stand the thought I lost her then. That I had something to do with it.' I hid my face in my hands.

'It made a mess of us all,' she said. 'All of us.' She got to her feet and leaned against the sink. 'Mum couldn't love us anymore. She was frightened to. Her child was murdered, for God's sake.' Her mouth twisted as she wept, and she struggled to speak. 'I've got cancer. Stage four.' I got up and stood in front of her; she collapsed against me. 'I'm dying, Peter Rabbit, I'm dying.' She kissed my face. 'I can't stand it we're so broken.'

I held onto her and remembered how she had tried to comfort me all those years ago, and how I had hated her for it. For the fact she wasn't Izzy.

After dark I went out into the garden. The clouds had blown away and stars glinted hard in the black sky. Some of them are burnt out, dead suns, but we still see their light travelling towards us. Time played its tricks here too; the smell of tobacco smoke and perfume drifted through the air. 'I'm going to stay a while,' I thought to myself. And then I said it out loud, just in case.

At the Royal Station Hotel

Isabel sent Matt a text using one of the phones they'd bought to arrange what she called 'our trysts'. Her company had booked a room for a client at the Royal Station Hotel. The client had cancelled the meeting, but it was too late to cancel the room.

'If you have a mind,' she'd typed, 'we can use it to spend the afternoon together.'

Buying the phones had been Isabel's idea. Cheap, pay as you go, good for calls and texts and not much else. Without even a security code, each phone only had the number of the other stored in its memory. She had thought it all through. If one of the phones were discovered they were to say they'd found it and didn't know what to do with it. They were never to use names, and should always delete texts after they'd read them. 'As an extra precaution,' she'd said, 'against getting caught.'

When they met in the lobby of the hotel Matt was in a good mood, and leaned against the counter while Isabel checked in. The receptionist was blonde and pretty. She spoke with a foreign accent and he looked at her name badge.

'Zofia,' he said. 'That's a pretty name.'

She looked up from the computer and smiled at him. He asked her where she was from.

'Poland. Krakow.'

'It's a lovely city,' he said, remembering, without wanting to, that he'd gone there with Wendy for the Christmas markets before they were married.

Zofia smiled at him again, and asked if they wanted one or two key cards for the room.

'One will do,' said Isabel. In the lift she pretended to be cross with Matt for flirting with the receptionist. 'Perhaps you'd rather be with her than me.'

They kissed in the lift, running their hands over each other's bodies, but when they got to the room, she told him to go into the en-suite and undress while she phoned her husband, to say she would be late home. It only took a minute.

'All done,' she said.

Matt came out of the bathroom wearing a towel around his waist. He let it drop to the floor, got into the bed and lay back with his hands behind his head to watch her undress.

'What?' she said, unhooking her bra.

'You look pleased with yourself.'

'I think we're rather good at this. Don't you?'

'What? Sneaking around and having sex?'

'It's called adultery, darling,' she said. 'It's a sin. And it's exciting. I like sneaking around. I like that it's a secret from everyone. It would be dull if it wasn't. It would just be routine. It would become like all the other things we do. And I like the sneaking around with our little burner phones.'

'Like spies, you mean?'

'It's the whole double life thing. Don't you like the buzz of it? Fiddling around the edges and finding ways to be together? I just love the build-up. The anticipation. I love how it makes the sex. It means we're just not putting up with the drudge. That's all. We should do a blog. Anonymous of course. A sort of adulterer's handbook.'

'I love you. You do know that. Don't you?' said Matt. 'Why don't we just confess all and be damned about the consequences?' But he knew he'd said too much, had come too close to being needy, which she never liked.

'Don't be silly. That wouldn't do at all. Think of the fallout.'

Isabel got into bed and sat astride him, which was how she liked to have sex, and afterwards they fell asleep.

Matt woke with his arm around her and reached for his watch on the night stand. It was after six. Later than he thought and time to go. He tried to wake Isabel, but something was wrong; her body was limp and heavy. He felt her wrist for a pulse, but he couldn't find one and thought it was because he didn't know how to. He put his ear to her chest to listen for a heartbeat, and then put his cheek above her mouth and nose to try and feel her breathe. His skin prickled, his own heart was beating too fast, and he felt dizzy, as if he was on the edge of a precipice. She was dead.

Informing the hotel or calling emergency services would mean everything would be out in the open. Wendy, he knew, would be vicious in her revenge. And who could blame her? It was betrayal pure and simple because it revealed an awful truth; the life he lived wasn't quite good enough. No, it wouldn't do at all to say the life you'd ended up with wasn't quite good enough.

And it didn't matter that he loved Isabel. In fact, he'd always loved her, since they'd first met at university. They'd even gone out together for a while, for him a heady fortnight of love and frantic sex. She laughed when he told her he wanted to be a poet because she said there was no money in it. It was Steve who stole her from him, pushy, going somewhere Steve Race who beguiled her away.

That was the turning point, what set him on the path to the life he had now; a wife and two children and a career in advertising and now in PR, with a company car and a Rolex and ski-ing holidays and all the other things he bought to console himself. Perhaps the affair was revenge for the way things had turned out.

Matt flushed the condom they'd used down the toilet, got dressed and made sure he had everything that belonged to him. He arranged Isabel's head on the pillow and smoothed her hair. She looked asleep and at peace, and he kissed her on the lips before leaving the room.

He took the fire stairs to avoid using the lift. At the bottom of the stairwell, he looked through the glass pane in the door, waiting until the receptionist was busy with customers and walked quickly with his head turned away from the desk, hoping to deny her another glimpse of his face, so as to linger less in her memory.

When he got home Wendy was having a row with their eldest, Alice. Something about a party she wanted to go to. 'But I'm thirteen,' he heard her say. Wendy was laying down the rules. 'If she went,' she said, her father would pick her up at eleven o'clock. But, of course, Alice wanted it to be midnight.

Matt watched the little drama play out. He was having trouble falling into step with what was expected of him. They were both demanding something from him, giving him his cues and waiting for him to remember his lines. He heard 'Dad?' and 'Say something to your daughter' and found the words in his mouth before he'd even thought them.

'You're right, Alice. You're thirteen. As in "only thirteen". And as midnight is the bewitching hour, I'll pick you up at eleven thirty. If that's not good enough…'

The house phone rang and Wendy went into the hall to answer it. Matt listened to the sound of her voice, trying to make out the words. It was Steve, he knew, trying to track down Isabel because she hadn't come home.

Wendy didn't think it meant that much. She said Isabel had probably gone late night shopping after work. And Matt knew it was something Isabel used as an excuse to cover some of the times they spent together, in a country pub, or parked up overlooking a beach or in some other secluded spot where they could have sex with the windows of the car steaming up. Sometimes she went out and bought something at lunchtime, a top or a skirt or a pair of trousers she didn't really like, to have something to show, something she would have to take back to the shop the next day.

Matt poured himself a whisky. He needed a drink to steady himself, and he wanted to have something to do with his hands. Wendy was surprised he was having a drink so early in the evening and he said he'd had one of those days. He was working on a publicity campaign for the university and said they didn't really know what they wanted, and were proving to be a real pain.

'Never mind,' she said. 'You'll work it out. You always do.'

It was typical of Wendy; she was always dismissive of any problems he had with work. Now she was more interested in showing him some sofas she'd found online. She had a new project; giving the sitting room what she called 'a refresh'.

When Matt bent over her to look at the screen on her laptop, she said he was a bit stinky. He remembered breaking out into a sweat in the hotel room. Thinking she might smell Isabel on him, he knocked back the whisky and said he needed a shower. Really, he wanted to be alone. Up in the bathroom, even before the water washed over him, he started crying because Isabel was dead, and until a chambermaid went in to the hotel room the next morning, he was the only one who knew it.

The next day, Steve phoned him at lunchtime and said the police had been to see him and told him Isabel had been found dead in a room at The Royal Station Hotel. Matt thought he had made a good show of sounding incredulous; saying 'What?' and letting Steve do all the work.

'They say she was with someone,' said Steve. 'Another man.'

'You mean…she was killed?'

'They don't know. Won't know until the post-mortem…Oh, fuck. That means they're going to cut her up, aren't they?'

Steve started crying and all Matt could think to say was 'Oh, shit, mate.'

'The bastard just left her there.'

'And no one knows who he is?'

'Some bastard. Leaving her like that.'

Matt didn't like the way Steve put it. He felt bad enough about running off the way he had. And that's how he thought about it; he'd run off. Fled the scene like a criminal. It had been important to keep the affair a secret and Isabel had been right, it added to the excitement. What good would it do to come clean about the whole thing now? In some ways what she called the drudge was all they had. The affair had been a fantasy, a relief from the frustrations of the dull necessities of life.

Steve's parents had come up from Nottingham to help him look after the children. He turned up at Matt and Wendy's a couple of nights later in the middle of a thunderstorm. Matt thought it was as if Steve had art directed the scene; hair plastered to his skull; his suit soaked through. He'd been drinking on his own in the town, he said and had never felt so alone, and didn't know where else to go because he didn't want the kids to see him like this. He knew he should be with them but he was all chewed up about things. Things, he said, he didn't understand.

Wendy hugged him and said he was always welcome, and it's at times like this people get to know who their friends really are. Matt poured him a glass of whisky. He didn't know what to say, but he needn't have worried because Steve did all the talking. About how he didn't know what to do, or how to help the kids deal with their mother's death. How he didn't know how he was going to cope without Isabel in his life.

'I mean, I'm finding it hard to process,' he said.

Matt thought that even now Steve had more of Isabel than he had ever had, because he could grieve for her openly, in a way Matt couldn't. He remembered how desolate he'd felt all those years ago when she'd finished with him. But there was some grim satisfaction when Steve got to the fact that she had been with another man when she died.

'I thought she was happy, you know,' he said. 'I really did. We'd done such a good job with the kids, and we've got a lovely house.'

'It is a lovely house,' said Wendy.

'And we'd just got the little place in France sorted out. I mean, I don't understand. Why was she unhappy enough to be seeing someone else?'

'Maybe it's true what they say,' said Wendy. 'How you never really know anyone.'

And as she said it, Matt realised the power there was in having a secret, in that no one really knew him either. It gave him a freedom. Perhaps it was what Isabel had meant, that they had given themselves a space to be someone else, not just the person who had ended up with that job, in that marriage, with those kids, all because of the cards life had dealt them, the paths they'd been forced to take. There was a space, if one dared to take it, to be someone else.

Matt knew he should have got rid of the burner phone, but it still nestled in the inside pocket of his jacket. When he was alone, he would take it out and look at it expectantly, willing it to vibrate and for a text to appear on its tiny screen. It was the only connection he had with Isabel; it had become a fetish object to remember her by.

But it was a dangerous thing to do. He was with Wendy in the supermarket for the wretched weekly shop, when the bloody phone started to vibrate in his pocket. It caught him off guard, and all he could think to do was to push ahead with the trolley, with Wendy calling after him until it rang out. Afterwards, he realised the police would have given Steve Isabel's things. After finding the phone in her handbag, he would be compelled to call the number stored in its memory.

Later, after he'd dropped Josh at the sports centre for his weekly football practice, he parked a few streets away and used the phone to call Isabel's number. Steve answered and shouted down the line, demanding to know who he was and calling him names. Matt didn't say anything; he ended the call and switched the phone off.

The media picked up on the case of a woman found dead in a room at The Royal Station Hotel. Cause of death to be determined. Police were looking for a man and Matt wondered if Zofia, the receptionist, would recognise him. After the story made the local television news, he dreamt a dream he hadn't had since he was a boy, a dream he supposed everyone had, of finding himself naked in a public place. He felt compelled to start walking past the hotel at odd times during the days that followed, testing the limits of chance, playing with his own safety. Some of the old excitement of the affair had returned when he'd used the phone to call Steve.

And then he saw Zofia, standing on the steps of the hotel smoking a cigarette. She looked different, less congenial, as she smoked and stared back at the men gawping at her in her short uniform skirt. Matt made a point of keeping his head turned towards her as he walked by. He smiled at her but she didn't smile back. She gave him the same look of disdain she was giving to the other men who looked at her. Because she was pretty, men felt they had the right to flirt with her and she would have to be pleasant about it if she wanted to keep her job.

It was so commonplace; why would she remember him any better than the rest? He was just an everyman, the kind she saw everyday as she handed out key cards and gave out the times for breakfast when they checked in, or asked if they'd had anything from the mini-bar, or watched a movie or porn on one of the pay to view channels when they checked out.

He walked down to the Quayside and watched the river for a while. The water, flowing towards the sea, was oblivious to his problems. It didn't care. Nor did it judge him. Nor did the grey sky nor the wheeling birds nor the guano-spattered bridge. He took the burner phone out of his pocket, switched it on and tapped out a text message with his thumbs, 'She died in my arms and I loved her.' After he'd sent it, he dropped the phone in the river and walked back up into the town.

That evening Wendy showed him the front page of the local newspaper with the headline 'IS THIS THE MYSTERY MAN IN HOTEL DEATH?' There was a photograph, a blurred image from the hotel's CCTV. He took the paper from her.

'Hard to make anything out, isn't it?' he said, putting the paper down. 'It could be anyone.'

The Dark Wood

The lift had a digital lock. The code was the same one you needed to get in and out of the building. Remembering it was a test, like those questions they used to ask Dad about what year it was and the name of the prime minister. Questions he doesn't know the answers to anymore. I tapped in the four-digit number and went up to the first floor.

*

I was driving at ninety miles an hour. I looked at the clock on the dash and thought, perhaps I won't be late. But the wind beat hard around the car. The rhythm numbed me. My eyes wanted to close. I slowed to seventy and moved into the nearside lane, lowering the window to let cold air blast onto my face. A road sign. Twenty-one miles to the services at Ferrybridge. Fifteen or twenty minutes. I only had to stay awake for fifteen or twenty minutes.

But by Ferrybridge I was bushed. I couldn't make sense of the signs for the car park. And the arrows painted on the road had been worn away. I took the turn at the last moment, and too fast, struggling to control the car as it lurched over the potholes. I eventually found a space near the main building, turned off the engine, reclined the seat and closed my eyes. Ten, fifteen minutes would do it. Then I'd be as right as rain. Then I'd call him.

I dreamt I was in the dark wood. The trees reached up and blocked out the sky. I was walking beside my father. He was stooped over, holding himself up with a walking pole. He looked like Moses in those pictures we used to look at in Sunday school. He was mumbling but I couldn't hear what he was saying.

Something woke me. The hard ringing of a telephone. The Old Phone ringtone I had chosen from my mobile's menu for its suggestion of traditional values. Of reliability. I fumbled to answer it.

'Well,' said the voice, 'I'm sitting here at Ferrybridge Services. Where the fuck are you?'

'I've just got here,' I said. 'Roadworks.'

'Roadworks, my arse. You're half an hour late.'

I got out of the car and struggled to get into my jacket as it flapped about in the wind, unable to find the sleeves with my arms. Twisting and turning in a mad dance, I finally pulled it on. I grabbed my laptop case and thought, here we go.

*

The smell was a fetid mix of stale urine and the air freshener they use to try and mask it. My father wasn't in his room. One of the care assistants and I started to look for him. He was wandering, which they say is what he does now. We found him on another corridor, stooped over and pushing the walker along with grim determination.'Hello, Dad,' I said, and touched his shoulder. 'It's me, Dad. It's Paul.'

But he ignored me and kept shuffling along. I kept pace with him. He was talking to himself, and I bent down to try and hear what he was saying.

*

Laurence Davis was sitting by the window. Some overweight men look comical, but not Laurence. He was just big. He'd marked out his territory on the table with a very large cup of coffee, a Maximo, an A5 notebook, two mobile phones and his open laptop. He'd taken his jacket off. He was wearing gold cufflinks and his tie hung over his gut.

I circled around to the coffee concession and bought a Largo, which is really just a regular-sized Americano. Then I went over to Laurence's table and put my jacket on the back of a chair, my coffee and laptop on the space he'd left for me, and sat opposite him. I got out my notebook to show I was ready for the meeting. He looked up at me from whatever he was looking at on his computer, and I took a big gulp of the coffee.

'You still like the Audi?' he said, tilting his chin out towards the car park. From where he was sitting he could see my car, and I realised he must have watched me sleeping. He let me take that in, smiling to himself as he turned the laptop round so that I could see what was on the screen.

'Look at that,' he said. It was a picture of a blonde woman wearing a bikini and leaning against a rock on a beach. Her name was Olga; she was 36 years old and she was an Aquarius.

'Very attractive,' I said.

'Russian women,' he said, 'know how to look after themselves. Desperate to meet men. They're not like the women here. Do you know that in Russia there are ten million…That's right, ten million more women than men.' He took a swig of his coffee. 'She's not *very attractive*…she is *fucking* beautiful.'

'You looking for love then, Laurence?' I put an edge in my voice, but he didn't seem to notice, or care.

'I'm Internet dating. It's the only way to meet women. Most of them are just gagging for it. Got some Viagra online as well.

Fantastic stuff. Puts the blood where you need it. When you need it. But these Russian women are something else. You still married?'

'Yup.'

He looked at me and I looked away to avoid his eyes.

Behind him a young woman of about twenty was sitting alone, smiling to herself as she worked the keypad of her phone. I could see her legs under the table. They were tanned a deep brown and reached up from the floor towards a faded denim miniskirt. She stretched them out as if she were a cat. I felt guilty, as if my eye was pressed to a keyhole. As if I shouldn't have been looking.

Laurence turned to see what I was looking at.

'A bit young for you, Mr. Married Man.' He looked again. 'Mind you, I'd give her one.' He had seen himself in me and I hated him for it. 'Sales figures,' he said. 'Let's talk about sales figures.'

*

Pat, Dad's social worker, came out of the lift holding a long white stick. She was blind and her guide dog was a Golden Labrador with sad brown eyes.

'Look at that dog.' I said to my father.

'What dog?' he said.

*

Laurence called my name.

'I'm sorry,' I said, 'but I was somewhere else.'

'Last year you were selling quite well. The year before that, really well. But not now. You must be feeling the pinch in your commission. No romantic trips to Paris with the missus.'

He was right. Once I would have been getting congratulated about my performance. Second, or at least third biggest order book in the company. And Laurence and I would be sneaking looks at the blonde in the miniskirt and giggling. Give her one? You bet.

Greetings cards should sell themselves. Births, birthdays, marriages, deaths. And the rest of it. New house, new job. The whole of life marked out in little celebrations. And someone somewhere was opening a card and a cheap bottle of Prosecco. Laughter. And some tears. But my heart wasn't in it. The wholesalers didn't want to buy all that stuff from a man whose joie de vivre wasn't jumping up and down in front of them. And the stuff wasn't as good as it used to be, but no one wanted to hear that.

*

'Look at that dog,' said my father suddenly.

I bent to stroke it, to feel the warmth of its animal body. Pat's eyes, visible through half closed lids, flitted from side to side.

'Are you alright, Paul?'

'We're not getting on today,' I said.

*

In a daze I looked out of the window at the white sky and saw black birds wheeling above the car park. I heard them through the glass. The craw-craw of crows looking for whatever had died or been killed.

'A murder of crows,' I said. 'Evil fuckers.'

'They're not evil,' said Laurence. 'They keep the world clean of rotting flesh. And dead meat.'

I looked at those legs again, golden against the pale blue of the floor. I realised, with disappointment, that my interest wasn't sexual. My eye was up against that keyhole to spy on her youth and her optimism, and I saw the distance between us.

I wanted to say, I've lost it, Laurence. I wanted to blurt it out and I wanted him to use all his powers to make it better. I wanted him to take me to a bar so we could get drunk together, laugh like old mates and chat up women.

What was he going to say? Hand back the car, the contract phone and cut me off from everything? The road, the mission. For fuck's sake.

'We can't count on what happened yesterday. It's today that counts,' he said.

I used to see myself as some kind of western hero roaming this part of the country, along the motorways, the A roads and the B roads, searching out the wholesalers. I had built up a territory of customers. It was something I owned and I was angry that he was going to ignore it all. I stood up to leave.

'Paul,' he said. 'I'm not the bad guy here.' My laptop was nearly back in its case as I looked over at him. 'I let you sleep, Paul. For at least half an hour.'

I made a kind of upside-down smile and mouthed an okay. I sat down again.

'I've got to tell you how it is, haven't I? You must know that you're costing the company.' He looked me straight in the eye. 'Basic salary, car, phone, etcetera. Can you get it back, Paul? The magic?' He looked away and back again. 'Three months. Can you turn it around in three months?'

*

I switched off the engine and the wipers stopped mid-wipe. Thick drizzle covered the windscreen and the building opposite distorted into a grey blur. There used to be something magical about these trading estates. They were scruffy and uncared for even in the beginning, but there'd always been the smell of money about them. And I'd felt part of it. Now they were just worn-out places, at the edges of towns that had seen better days.

Betta-price Gifts and Giftware was a single storey building with a crumbling brick façade topped with peeling woodwork. The young Asian woman on reception was wearing a hijab, and a short floral dress over jeans. Abdul Choudary seemed to be pleased to see me, dressed as ever in a suit with a cardigan underneath, which he wore even in the summer. We went into his wood panelled office and the receptionist brought us coffee in mugs on a tray. It was always Nescafe at Betta-price Gifts and Giftware.

'When I came to this country,' Abdul told me, 'Nescafe was a mark of English sophistication. Very exciting for a young man from Pakistan. Now my son tells me that it is rubbish, for old men only. It is all cappuccinos and Americanos now. I am sorry, if all this time I have been giving you a very bad beverage experience.'

I laughed at his joke. Abdul had started out as a newsagent in Bradford during the 1970s and had branched out into wholesale, supplying the sector with giftware and greetings cards. I had known him for nearly twenty years. He leaned back in his chair and put his hands together.

'I am retiring,' he said. 'My son, Rushdi will see about the order today.'

Rushdi was a handsome young man with a close-cropped beard. He wore a blue and white striped shirt with white collar and cuffs, the cuffs turned back to show off a large wristwatch. He was a man of the moment; I could tell that by the way he shook my hand. He looked through my portfolio cases on his father's desk. He flicked the pages quickly, scanning them half-heartedly. I could tell that he was only going through the motions for his father's sake.

'Some of these cards are too old fashioned for our customers. Your company needs to move with the times. Newsagents don't just sell to old English ladies who are happy with pictures of racing cars and fishing rods for their grandsons' birthdays. They need to compete with the internet and the supermarkets.'

He looked at me and I didn't know what to say.

'Just a small order,' said Abdul. 'For the few old ladies who still need that sort of thing.' I got out my order book. 'You look tired, Paul.'

I shrugged.

*

I showed my father a photograph of a young man in uniform. He stretched his hand towards it, running the tips of his fingers over the mouth. Over the toothy smile.

'He looks as if he might have been me.'

'It is you, Dad. It is you. When you were in the army.'

'Oh yes,' he said. 'I remember. Funny teeth.'

*

I booked into the Premier Inn at Wakefield and called home.

'How are you?' asked Sue.

'He gave me three months. After twenty years.'

'Leave it, Paul. It's not worth it. Come home. Play golf. Walk the dog.'

I grunted and thought about the dark wood. And I remembered how it began. Retirement, losing interest. The plans that came to nothing because he couldn't be bothered anymore. Everything was too much trouble. What happened to the man in him? Where did he go?

'Emma's nearly finished her course. Ruth's getting married, for God's sake. Call it a day. You deserve it.'

'I'll think about it,' I said. 'How's the dog?'

'He's missing you. So am I. I love you.'

'I love you, too,' I said.

I threw the phone on the bed and lay down beside it. I looked around the room. There's meant to be something comforting about a hotel chain. Same colour scheme, same pictures. The same breakfast buffet and the same coffee. The same television sets and the same remote controls. They try to make everything bright and cheerful, and I winced at the thought. It looked like a lonely dinner and then to bed to read Bernard Cornwell, with a cup of cocoa from a sachet.

I went to the hotel restaurant and had steak and chips and a glass of wine. Then I had another glass. And when I'd drained that I went into the bar. The barman looked bored. There was hardly anyone there, just a couple of women in their thirties, who didn't even notice that I was in the room, and a man standing at the bar.

I ordered a large glass of red and he turned to me.

'You in sales?'

I swung an imaginary golf club and made a clicking sound with my tongue.

'Hole in one.' I'd had a drink. I was back on form.

'It's not what it used to be,' he said.

'You're telling me,' I said and looked at him. He might have been a mirror image. Overweight, middle-aged and wearing a dark blue suit with an open necked shirt. The tie would be lying on the bed in his room. Just like mine.

I bought him a drink and we went and sat down. We looked over at the two women.

'We're not even on their radar,' he said.

Neil was in pharmaceutical sales, and said that generic drugs were killing the business. I guess he meant he had to work harder for his commission, but I could tell he still had the fight in him.

He said he was going out for a smoke and I thought about the dark wood again. What was the date? Who was the prime minister? I followed Neil outside.

He was standing in the glow of the lights, blowing cigarette smoke into the night. 'Can you spare one of those?' I asked.

'I didn't think you smoked.'

'Used to. Gave up. Still think about it, though.'

'Once a smoker…' he said.

I lit the cigarette. It was like old times. The flush of alcohol and the bite of tobacco smoke on the back of my throat. I inhaled and, at that moment, remembered my first cigarette. When I was fourteen years old a girl in a miniskirt and a push up bra had offered me one. I had taken it and put the filter tip between my lips as she held up a flaring match. I sucked in tentatively and tasted sulphur in the acrid smoke. I blew it straight out.

'You're meant to inhale it,' she said. I did and all of a sudden, the world turned upside down as, in a dizzy spin, I fell over. This happened now as the nicotine rushed to my head, and I went straight down, landing on my arse like a circus clown. A pratfall.

*

A woman was shredding a tissue, the fragments falling onto the floor like giant snowflakes. I looked around at the other residents. Some were moving slowly and wordlessly, some were sitting and staring at the floor, or sleeping in their chairs, bent and awkward, with gaping mouths. The laughter and applause of a TV game show came from the set no one was watching, and I realised I was trying to breathe without smelling the air.

'Hello Dad. It's Paul. I'm your son.'

He studied me carefully. 'No,' he said, 'No, you're not.'

And I thought, that's it, I'm forgotten now. He leaned against the walker and looked at me.

'Some people have it,' he said, 'and some people don't.'

Acknowledgements

Writing requires hiding alone in a room for long periods of time, and I am eternally grateful to my patient and beloved wife Ailsa for putting up with the whole business. I would like to thank fellow writers Jamie Warde-Aldam and Tony Glover for their support over the years. Also, Tom Noble for lots of things and Wayne Gamble for his excellent design work.